Two Months Ago

Prologue

Instead of tears rolling down my cheeks, sweat breached my brow, smudging my make-up. The church where my mother's funeral service was being held was hot as Satan's balls. And I was caught between assuring flower arrangements were placed perfectly and comforting my little sister, Skye, through her melt down.

She wailed enough for the both of us. My tears weren't needed.

"Nova, can I help you with anything?" my best friend, Misa, asked as she approached me in all black.

"No, I'm good. Go check on Skye. Make sure she doesn't hyperventilate," I instructed, while nudging her toward my despondent sister.

"What about you? Are you sure you're okay?" she pried.

"I'm fine. We're missing some flowers. I have to go outside and check with the delivery guy." I attempted to walk away.

But she followed me. Everyone was being extra careful with me because none of them had seen me

2

break down in tears. I just didn't feel it. Grief hits people at different times, I guess.

With Misa on my heels, I stomped outside into the warm sun. My mother, Antoinette, was lucky to be laid to rest on a warm and lovely day.

"Excuse me, sir, we're missing a white rose reef arrangement," I spoke when I approached the man dressed in a blue jumpsuit. He was climbing back into the floral delivery van.

"I'm sorry, ma'am, that's all we have in the back. They didn't load any white rose reefs."

"That's unacceptable. I ordered and paid for it. I want it here," I thrashed. His brow furrowed, as he looked me up and down.

"That's an odd color for a funeral," he commented at my powder blue linen dress while digging for his cell phone in his pocket.

I didn't bother responding to his observation. Powder blue was perfect for a funeral. It was light and airy. And that was what I needed to be today. I needed to hold it together.

"Nova, what's going on?" Misa asked from behind me.

"I told you to check on my sister. Please, Misa. I'm fine!" I stressed to her. Defeated, she nodded and turned away back into the church.

When I returned to the deliveryman, he had slipped his phone back in his pocket. My stomach tightened in anticipation for what he had to say.

"I apologize for the inconvenience, Mrs. Shelton. I spoke with my boss and he's going to give you a full refund for the..."

"That is unacceptable! I paid you people to do a fucking job and you shortchanged me! This is my mother's fuckin' funeral!" I flipped out, surprising myself.

Before the man could part his lips to respond to me, I heard my soon to be ex-husband shout my name.

"Nova! Calm down, baby!" he shouted grabbing my arm and pulling me away from the delivery guy. He nodded to the man, cueing him to leave while he walked me to the corner, away from the crowd that had begun to form to see what the commotion was about.

My entire family and all my friends saw me go berserk on the deliveryman. Regret washed over me as I thought about how I blew my cool. All I wanted to do was to get through this funeral without showing much emotion.

But it was all too much.

"Baby, what is going on? Are you okay?" he asked, stroking my cheek.

The touch of his fingers to my perfectly beat face made my skin crawl. I had half a mind to bite him.

"Get your fucking hands off of me," I snarled between gritted teeth.

"I know that you're grieving. I know that you're upset and that's okay. I need you to let it out. Let it all out. You know that I'm here for you," he attempted to convince me. But I knew it was all lies and bullshit.

"Tyriq, get the fuck out of my face. Why are you even here?"

"Nova, I love you! I loved Ms. Toni. She was like a mother to me. Why are you being like this? What has gotten into you? You were fine when I saw you this morning."

"It's funny how quickly someone can change. Isn't it?" I asked cryptically before turning to walk away.

Yeah, I was fine when he last saw me earlier this morning. But that was before I found out the truth about him. A truth that I had to sort through along with the burial of my mother.

As I walked away from my husband, I weaved in and out of the sea of folks dressed in black. I was the only one that dared to wear a light color, aside from some of the children.

My blue dress stood out as I climbed the stairs to the church. I could feel the dozens of eyes burning into my backside as I approached the church's door. When I walked back in, my eyes landed on Skye, who was sprawled out on the closed part of the casket. She was banging her fists on the hard cover while yelling, "Please don't leave me."

I sighed, while watching the pathetic sight. You see, this was why I couldn't mourn. This heffa was doing more than enough.

She hollered to the top of her lungs as a couple of our cousins rushed to her side, attempting to pull her away. The veins in her balled fists throbbed while her tears poured.

She was a sad weakling, just like our mother.

Chapter 1

Nova

"You just need to leave him," I flatly said to Misa, while swirling pasta around my fork before stuffing it in my mouth.

"I can't! You know I can't." She sniffled, barely touching her lunch.

There we sat outside at Luciano's, an Italian eatery in downtown D.C., eating lunch and talking about her philandering husband.

Misa was a beautiful woman, but since getting married and spitting out a few babies, she had let herself go. I remembered telling her, she had to keep it tight, if she didn't want that fine ass husband of hers to look outside of home for some pussy.

But she didn't listen. She swore up and down he loved her for who she was no matter what.

My response was, "What does love have to do with his dick?"

Men can love you and still want to fuck other bitches. Your job is to keep him so satisfied so that he is too caught up in you to sleep around.

But Misa didn't keep up with her looks to keep him interested. And what the hell was her excuse? It wasn't like she had to work. My ass worked, sometimes 60 hour work weeks. And I still managed to keep my body looking good, hair done, food on the table, and pussy or mouth on his dick. Granted, I had no kids yet, but work took up just as much time.

"I just can't believe he would do this to me! I supported him through law school! If it weren't for me, he wouldn't even be an assistant district attorney. And he does this to me!" Her tears had dried, but the anger still lingered.

I paused from scarfing down the fettuccine alfredo that lay on my plate to look her in her sad eyes.

She had a cute round face, the color of burnt sienna. Her skin was so smooth and unblemished; it looked as if she were wearing foundation. But that was the only thing she had going for her.

The three babies she popped out for her asshole husband had left her skinny-fat. She never had much boobs or butt, but the babies made everything sag. Her naturally long hair was never done. She kept it swooped in a ponytail. And she stayed in baggy t-shirts and unflattering yoga pants.

I had tried to tell her before, but it never worked. And now wasn't the time. What she needed now was encouragement.

"Just leave him, Misa. You are beautiful, talented, and intelligent. You don't need him."

"I can't leave him. The kids are in really good daycares and I can't afford it without him. Where will I live? What will I drive? You know I signed a pre-nup."

Shaking my head, I took a sip of the ice water in my glass. Women were so dumb. This was why I could never be fully dependent on a man.

Sure, my husband and I were a power couple. But if he left, I would be okay. You had to have a career and never ever sign a pre-nup! If he cheated, you needed to be taking his ass to the cleaners.

"Is he only cheating with one girl? And do you know who it is?" I prodded.

"Yeah, that I know of. She's the only one who's been texting him and calling him. I finally followed him one day, and he went to a hotel to see her."

"You have to get rid of her. Just kill her ass," I joked while laughing. It lightened the mood, forcing Misa into giggling.

"I wish. That little bitch knows he's married yet she still runs around with him."

"I hate those kind of women! Side chicks and mistresses. Get your own man, you pathetic broads!" I fussed.

I really did hate those bitches. They break up homes every day. I know it's really the man's fault, but if there weren't so many of those hoes who willingly slept with married men, there wouldn't be nearly as big of a problem.

Sometimes, I wished all of those bitches would just die. I know that's terrible. I need help, pray for me. I laughed to myself.

"Well girl, I know you have to get back to work. I don't want to hold you up."

"Yeah, let me head back to the office so I can wrap up this press release. Maybe we can catch up this weekend for a spa day?" I suggested. With all the stress she was dealing with, she needed it.

"I'll see if I can get someone to watch the kids."

"Let me know," I replied, while we waited for the check to come.

***

After lunch, I sashayed down the crowded sidewalk to get back to my building. My leopard Loubous clicked along the cement, while I switched my curvy ass. Niggas broke their necks to catch a glimpse of the fat ass walking before them.

I was a naturally a thick girl. In spite of some of the cosmetic surgery I had I was definitely still considered a BBW. Right after college, I went and got liposuction around my midsection and had the fat transferred to my tits and my ass, giving me a bodacious hour-glass figure. I was thick in all the right places.

My butter pecan skin was flawless and glinted underneath the sun as I trekked back to my office. The black pencil skirt I wore hugged my hips, but the tan blouse I wore was much more modest.

I couldn't be in my office with my cleavage showing. My goal was to eventually become one of the vice presidents at the public relations firm. And I wasn't going to get there dressing like one of these thots.

"Welcome back Ms. Shelton," Ron, the security guard greeted me as I walked through the halls. He was always nice to me, trying to flirt.

"Hey Ron. And you know its Mrs., right?" I corrected him. I don't play that shit. I'm a married woman who is deeply in love with my man. I rock this diamond on my fourth finger with pride.

"Excuse me! I was just wishful thinking," he joked. Without verbally responding, I smirked and stepped on the elevator to the 12th floor, where I had my own office with a beautiful view of the city.

At only twenty-eight years old, I had made senior account executive at the firm, Ashworth Marketing. Which allowed me to lead some PR and marketing campaigns for a lot of heavy hitters that included beverage brands, apparel companies, and real estate.

Before going back into my lovely office, I stopped in the restroom to reapply my cherry colored lipstick. While in the bathroom, I primped my hair, which was cut in the mushroom bob style, similar to Rihanna's.

I went to my hairdresser weekly to keep the hairstyle looking perfect. I don't know who made up the lie that short hair was less maintenance. When you have a style like this, you have to keep your kitchen looking good.

After assuring my hair was perfect and my lips were on fleek, I settled back at my desk to complete the day.

"Hey Nova," Andrea, my manager, a vice president, said when she walked into my office.

"Hi Andrea, what's going on?"

"I just wanted to give you a kudos for the lovely job you did on the American leg of the Satori campaign. The stuff is flying off the shelves all over the country." Andrea referred to Satori wine, a Japanese wine company that hired Ashworth to do its marketing.

It was my first assignment as an account executive, and I had done a really good job.

"Thank you! I read the reports this morning. The sales are doing well."

"It's all because of you. Keep up the good work, lady. One day soon you'll be up there with me and the other big dogs," she chuckled.

"You know that's always been the goal." I smiled.

"I know and you're well on your way. I'm rooting for you," she replied before turning away.

"Oh and before I forget. Your bonus will be in this next paycheck and I'm sure you will be pleasantly surprised." She winked before exiting.

There was nothing like doing an amazing job and getting paid for it. As I read over the press release that I wrote for another client, my cell phone rang. It was my mother, Antoinette, also known as Toni.

"Sup ma," I answered with the phone pressed between my ear and my shoulder.

"Nova, I need you to come over tonight. I have a surprise I want to tell the family. Bring your husband," she gleefully said.

"It's a little short notice, don't you think?"

"Just come. It's very important. You know, Nova, you only have one mother. You need to treat me right..." She went on her extended rant about how I should treat her well since she was older and could die tomorrow. Rolling my eyes, I blocked her out. I hated when she did that shit.

"Fine, I'll be there. I'll talk to you later," I replied. As soon as I hung up, I phoned my husband. I hated interrupting him at work. He didn't need any distractions. Just like me, he was also one of the youngest people at his job in an upper management position.

My baby worked for one of the top real estate development firms in the area, Durden Development. Like I said, we were a power couple, striving to be the best in our careers and lead elite lives.

"Hey sweetie," he answered the call.

"Good afternoon, love. I won't hold you. Please meet me at my mother's house tonight. She said she had an important announcement and wants you there along with me."

"What? Is she pregnant?" He laughed at his own joke.

"Boy please. She better not be. As old as she is." I laughed back.

"You said it, not me." He continued to chuckle.

"You implied it. But can I count on you to be there?"

"Of course. I love you. I gotta run."

"Love you too, baby." I hung up and returned to work.

I loved my how my husband made an effort to be there for me.

Chapter 2
Tyriq

"Of course. I love you. I gotta run," I replied before hanging the phone up on my gorgeous wife.

But when I looked up from my cell phone, I was met with an evil eye and severe sucking of teeth.

"Don't be like that," I said to Kinasha, my assistant and secret jump off.

"I just hate how you do that shit in front of me. You see me sitting right here, yet you still answer your phone when she calls. It's disrespectful," she hissed while poking her bottom lip out.

These thots never knew how to stay in their place. I cleared my throat and shrugged it off, while returning back to our conversation.

"What was I saying again? Oh yeah, I need you to come with me to the meeting tomorrow at the Gardens. I need you to be my eyes and ears. You take really good notes, okay?"

"Uh huh, I'll be there. But seriously, Tyriq, why are you even still with her? I thought we had something special," she whined while biting down on her bottom lip.

Every time she did that shit, my dick jumped. If we didn't have so much work to do, I would lock my office door and bend that ass over my desk, like I'd done hundreds of times.

"Because she's my wife," I flatly stated.

I know it sounds fucked up, but I do love my wife. But we got married too young and I'm not ready to stop getting pussy. I loved a variety of women. My wife was thick and had sexy short hair.

But Kinasha was petite with long hair. I loved tossing her little ass around and watching her tiny pussy swallow all ten inches of my dick. Her honey colored skin looked good against my deep chocolate flesh. Whenever I hit it from behind, I got to tangle my fingers in her hair while pounding her little pussy.

If she could shut up about my wife, we would be fine.

"I want to see you more, though. You get so busy..." she began to ramble.

"Fine, I'll make more time for you. You know you the best, baby. I care for you and love that pussy." I was careful to never say that I loved her, because I didn't. I was also careful to never give her money. What I made went back to my household with my wife.

"Oh, I know you do," she whispered, while spreading her legs so that I could catch a glimpse of her pink center.

"Damn, you better put that away. My door ain't locked."

"I don't give a fuck, let them watch." She sat across from my desk, rubbing her clit with one hand while sucking on her other finger. She simulated a blow job on her fingers, causing me to get rock hard.

"Seriously, Kinasha, go back to work. I'll break you off later."

"Fine, boss. I'll go back to work. But are you coming through tonight?"

"Nah, I have to go to a family thing."

There she went with that sucking her teeth shit. "You missed my birthday yesterday. And now you're telling me I can't see you tonight either?"

"We'll fuck again soon. And trust me, it will be worth the wait."

"Okay, baby," she said as she walked away.

Taking a few deep breaths, I waited for my dick to go soft so that I could get back to work. Durden Development was going through a lot of changes and if I wanted to continue to move up in the company I had to be able to rock with those changes.

I was on a mission to become partner in this company or open my own development firm. With my wife inspiring me, I made it through college and grad school at the top of my classes. And now I was making well over 100k.

It was as if we had it all: a mini mansion in Bowie, Maryland, three luxury cars between the two of us, a pair of Shih Tzus, and a timeshare in Jamaica. The only thing that was missing was children. Which didn't bother me much because I didn't think we had time for them yet.

Eventually, I want kids after I get this shit out my system. I can't stop fucking around and having kids would get in the way of that.

While I scanned the finance report on my computer screen, my office phone beeped. Looking at the caller ID, I could see that it was Kinasha.

"What's up," I greeted after pressing speakerphone.

"Cole Barnes is here to see you. I know he doesn't have an appointment, but he said it's urgent."

My temples throbbed at hearing his name.

"Send him back," I sighed. I did not feel like dealing with this nigga Cole, who I knew from the hood as Chop.

In a matter of moments the doorknob to my office turned and in walked the nigga from my sordid past.

"Wsup Chop." I stood and extended my hand to him.

He shook it before sitting down in the chair that Kinasha's sexy ass once sat in.

"Mr. Shelton! This is a nice set up you have going on here."

"Cut to it, why are you here?" I asked. I used to work the corners back in the day with Chop. We were both on the come up but now he was the kingpin. That could've been my life but I preferred to go straight. I'm too fucking pretty to be in prison. I used that drug money to pay for tuition and the rest is history.

"Damn nigga. I ain't seen you in a few years. Not since you got this cushy corporate job and that thick ass wife."

"Keep my wife out your fuckin' mouth," I barked.

"Whateva, nigga. I ain't come here for all of that. I came here because I need a favor."

"What kind of favor? I don't owe you shit."

"The hell you don't. It was my connect that helped you pay for grad school. If you didn't know me you woulda been broke and not able to even afford your degrees
that got you here."

He was right. He used to cop from one particular connect that used to keep us laced. I never got the opportunity to meet the connect but Chop was still doing business with him.

"Just get to it. What the hell do you want?"

"You know The Gardens over on the south side?" he asked, referring to some historic projects in the city.

"Yeah, my company working on putting a bid on that," I replied.

"I know, that's why I'm here. I need y'all to drop that shit."

"Nigga, have you lost your mind? You want us to drop our bid on that prime real estate?" I looked at him with confusion. The favor that he wanted me to perform was absurd.

"Yes, drop the bid. This gentrification shit is sucking the soul out of our city." He leaned into the chair, eyeing me like a hawk.

"Since when do you care about social issues? I thought all you were about is your dollas."

"That is all I'm about. I get a lot of my dollars from The Gardens. In fact, one of our traps is there. Which is why I need for no one to buy that property and build new fancy condos in its place."

Yep, this nigga had lost his mind.

"Chop, I can't help you. There's nothing I can do about The Gardens being sold." I shook my head as I eyed him.

He had an unnerving scar that ran down his cheek. To my knowledge, no one knew how he got the scar. But we all knew how he got the nickname.

When he was about 11, he caught his stepfather molesting his little sister. Later that night while the man was sleeping, Chop snuck into his room with a machete and severed his head.

He spent the next few years in juvi until he was 18. When he got out we started slinging together. But I went to college and later to grad school. Ain't no retirement plans for drug dealers. And I'm trying to live my life to its fullest.

"You can convince your company to drop the bid. So do it. I don't need any more explanations. I came in here and asked nicely. Don't let me get ugly," he barked.

"Quiet your damn voice. This is a place of business. All that shit might work in the trap but this is a company," I chastised him. I could see the fury brewing within him.

"Is no your final answer?" he questioned me as if I were going to change my mind.

"No is my final answer. That's not how shit works around here. Besides, I don't have the power to tell them to drop a bid that will bring the company tens of millions of dollars."

He tilted his head back and released an evil chuckle that eventually progressed to him clapping.

"Did I say something funny?" I thrashed. My patience had run thin and I wanted him out of my fuckin' office.

"Yeah, you funny. You one funny nigga," he said in between laughing.

"How is that?"

"You don't have no power. You moved all that weight back in the day just to become a monkey in a suit."

My abs tightened while my palms began to sweat. If I were light enough you would have been able to see my skin burn red. This nigga had the audacity to insult me, while I was out here trying to live a decent life.

"Well, what does it say about you that you have to come and ask a monkey in a suit for help," I slickly replied.

His face went stone cold.

"I would tread lightly if I were you."

"How about you tread your ass up out my office. This monkey in a suit has real work to do. Go back to the trap where your ass belongs."

Standing, he brushed his True Religion jeans to release any wrinkling. He let out a snicker that grated my nerves before replying.

"This won't be the last time you see me," he spoke before turning towards the door and heading out of my office.

Once he left, I let out a sigh of release. I knew not to ignore Chop's threats, but what could he really do to me? I knew too many of his secrets for him to try me. And I doubt if he would kill me because my brothers would react and blood would spill in these streets.

That nigga knows that. And he doesn't want a war.

I leaned back into my cushiony leather office chair and caught a glimpse of the photo that sat on my desk. It was a picture of Nova and me on our wedding day. She looked so beautiful that day and I vowed to give her whatever she wanted. Which reminded me, I had to get some more work done so I could go to her mother's house this evening.

Chapter 3

Aoki

The wind whipped through my lengthy tresses as I sped down 495, racing to Tyson's Corner. Today I was taking my home girl, Skye, shopping. On the way there we bumped that new Usher song "No Limit."

Together we sung along to the radio:

"Make you say uh, no limit
Got that Master P, no limit baby
Give you that black card, no limit
Just know when you roll with a nigga like me
There's no limit baby."

"Bitch, this is my song!" I hollered over the loudness of the wind.

"I love it too!" she agreed.

I looked over at Skye, who resembled a high fashion model. The girl had a pair of toned long legs that made everyone gawk at them. Including my ass.

In fact, that's how we met. We were on campus at GW when I spotted her across the walkway. I marched right up to her little shy ass and asked what kind of workouts does she do.

She said she didn't work out but that she was a dancer and that was her minor while her major was education. I chatted her up about other things, and from there we became close. But that was three years ago. Since then, I'd dropped out of school while she stayed behind.

"This whip is fly. How in the hell can you afford this?" Skye questioned, while her fingers trailed along the buttery interior of my Mercedes Benz E-Class convertible.

"I got myself a sponsor. Well, actually several sponsors." I watched her roll her eyes before erupting into laughter.

"You're crazy, bitch!" She shook her head.

"No, you're the crazy one. You're struggling in college to get a degree that don't even guarantee that you'll get a job. While I'm sitting pretty in this ride. I live in a cute condo. My nails and hair stay done. And my clothes cost the same amount as your room and board."

"That's because you're hoeing." She rolled her eyes as I turned off my exit.

"And you're fucking for free. What's your point?"

"It's not right, Aoki. What happens when you're too old to use your looks to get a man?"

"Bitch, get real. I have decades before that happens. And eventually, I'll marry some rich, ugly man who will be grateful to have me. And besides, I save for a rainy day." I smirked.

As I drove towards the mall, my phone rang.

"Skye, tell me who that is." I don't text nor talk while driving. My cousin, Mimi, died in a car accident from doing that. I've been spooked ever since.

"It says X. Is that one of your men?" she poked while laughing.

"Sure is, put that on speaker phone," I commanded.

"Hey baby," I answered while steering my car into the mall's parking lot.

"Bitch, this ain't baby! This is his wife. And you better stay away from my husband, you little slut! If I catch you out in public, I'm going to slice your fucking face."

"Whatever, you soggy pussy ass hoe. Slice my face, your husband will be paying for the cosmetic surgery, like he pays my rent, bitch. Go learn to suck dick."

"Hang up," I mouthed to Skye. Doing as I suggested, she ended the call.

"Oh my god, girl! That's ridiculous. You're sleeping with married men?"

"Yes I am, honey. Those are usually the best ones. They don't want much of your time, but they are willing to give you whatever you want as long as you stroke their ego."

"But his wife. You don't feel bad about what you're doing to her?"

Skye was so damned naïve. How is it possible that no one has schooled her on how life works?

"First of all, I'm not doing anything to her. Her husband is. Second of all, it's not my fault she can't keep her man satisfied. It surely isn't my fault that no one told her the truth about men and cheating."

"And what's that?" Skye asked while unbuckling her seatbelt once I parked.

"There are two different kinds of women. The one he cheats on and the one he cheats with. I decided long ago after watching my mother deal with my hoe of a father, that I was going to be the other woman. I watched her stay up night after night waiting for him to come home. And in the end when he died, a bunch of baby mother bitches came for his will."

"Why? You're selling yourself short." Her big brown doe eyes looked at me as if I were crazy.

"No, the wife and the girlfriend are selling their selves short. They give their all to these dogs. And yes, all men are dogs. They give their all and these men just take from them. Take their youth, beauty, money, and lives. And all they have to show for it is stretch marks, snotty nosed kids, and a picket fence. While the other woman keeps her youth and beauty and has several of those niggas in rotation. The key is to not fall in love."

"I don't believe in that. I think love and marriage is a beautiful thing. I look forward to it one day."

"Well, good luck. In the meantime, you should get you a sponsor. You're too cute to let that go to waste."

"I'd rather work for my things."

"Suit yourself." I shrugged as looked in the visor's mirror. My reflection was sexy.

My skin was café au lait colored, and I had a pair of chinky eyes, courtesy of my Asian heritage. My mother was Japanese while my father was Jamaican. My high cheekbones complemented my pouty mouth and small nose. Long black, curly hair cascaded down my back.

It was the type of hair bitches paid hundreds of dollars for, but it grew right from my scalp. My body was built like my father's family, curvy and thick. My breasts were small, about a handful. But what I lacked in breasts, I made up for in ass. Yep, I had a real big ass.

Sometimes, I considered getting a boob job; I was sure one of my sponsors would pay for it. But to be honest, surgery scared the shit out of me. And since I'd never had complaints about my tits, I let the thought of getting work on them go.

We got out of the car and headed towards the mall. Skye and I turned heads wherever we went. Her mocha skin was complemented with reddish undertones. Dark brown wavy hair stretched past her shoulders, while baby hair framed her pretty face. She reminded me of Chilli from TLC, but taller.

If I were her, I certainly wouldn't be in college while working as a waitress at Friday's, struggling to get by. But to each its own.

As we bounced in and out of boutiques, she got a call.

"Hey ma," she answered while we both walked towards Cinnabon. "Tonight? No, I don't have plans. Okay, I'll see you later."

"What was that about?" I questioned just before ordering us both Cinnabons.

"My mother said that she has a major announcement tonight. She wants me and my sister there."

"Uh uh, Ms. Toni! She can't be cutting into our shopping time." I had never met her mother or her sister but Skye talked about them all the time.

"I'm so sorry, we can come back tomorrow." She smiled, causing me to roll my eyes.

This bitch is lucky. I had to be back on our side of town anyway for a date with X. Fuck what his wife was talking about. It was time for him to give me my monthly allowance.

"Fine, let's roll. But you have to drive."

"That works."

Together we walked out of the mall while scarfing down our sweet treats.

Chapter 4
Skye

After Aoki's crazy ass dropped me off at my apartment, I jumped into my hoopty and dashed towards my mother's house.

I raced to my mother's house. My mind was riddled with anticipation of what her secret could be.

On the way there, I prayed that she would announce that she won the lottery because she and I are broke as hell.

My senior year of college starts in about a month and I still have no clue how I'm going to pay my tuition. The first three years my tuition was covered by an academic scholarship I had, but I lost it when my GPA dipped down to 2.5 last year, for two semesters in a row.

That was my own fault, though. I had gotten caught up with a d-boy named Chad which had me completely unfocused. After catching him cheating on me a couple of times, I finally decided to call it quits. And of course he did not take it lightly.

He started to stalk me, showing up at my dorm room and classrooms. Day after day he would blow up my phone, leaving me messages. At first they were sweet but then they devolved into threats, which forced me to get a part-time job so I could get an apartment off campus.

Finally, I moved to a studio apartment off of Georgia Ave. and he had no clue where I was living. I stopped hanging out at my old spots and had to go to class in a disguise. Eventually, he quit calling and stalking. But at times, I still felt unsafe.

Needless to say, I will never date a thug or a d-boy ever again. In fact, I don't even want a young nigga. I want someone older and more mature. And he has to have a legit job, making good money. No less than six figures. Until I find that mythical king, I shall remain single and focused on getting out of school.

As I cruised down the street in my 1999 Toyota Camry, I considered what Aoki had shared with me earlier today. Was I broke enough to stoop to her antics? Nah, I'll keep working like I am. Eventually it will pay off. If I can just make it through this last year of school, I'll be fine.

When I arrived at my mother's townhouse in Oxon Hill, MD, I pulled into the parking lot and checked my make-up before getting out the car. My skin still looked on point, and my lip gloss was popping. After toying with my baby hair, I leapt out of the car and headed towards my mother's door.

There was a bunch of random niggas sitting on the stoop to the house next to her, eying me as if I were juicy steak. I lifted my head high and kept it moving. Those little boys are the equivalent of thots. Thirst niggas.

"Ay ma, let me talk to you. Can I get your number?" one of the boys asked. I ignored him because what reason did I have to speak.

While I placed the key into the door, the same jerk yelled out, "Stuck up bitch."

I shrugged.

"Damn right, I'm stuck up. I have standards and you don't meet them."

Without giving him an opportunity to respond, I opened the door and emerged into my mother's living room where she sat on the couch alone.

"Hey ma," I said when I walked towards her. With a huge smile on her face, she stood and hugged me.

My mother and I had always been much closer than she and Nova. I'd seen this woman struggle with two kids, without the men to help her take care of them.

Nova's father died before she was born. And my father wanted nothing to do with my mother or me when they found out I was coming. It's funny how men can lay down and make a baby, yet not take on the responsibility.

We were always very poor growing up but she did the best that she could do. Unfortunately, she didn't have much help. Her relationships didn't work out and always left her even more broken hearted than before. Yet, she pressed on and did her best with us.

When my grandmother died, she left her this house, which was mostly paid off. But before living here, we lived in The Gardens, one of the city's worst projects. A place Nova and I vowed to escape.

"What is this surprise that you have to share?" I asked.

"Not now. We have to wait for your sister and I have another guest that's coming. Go and grab you something to drink and eat from the kitchen."

"No thank you. I don't want anything."

Before she could reply, the doorknob turned and in walked Nova.

"Where is Tyriq?" Ma asked her.

"Damn, can I get through the door? You didn't even greet me. The first thing out your mouth is where is my husband," Nova hissed before walking further into the house.

I loved my sister but she was so damned bitchy sometimes.

"Watch your mouth when you're in my house!" my mother yelled at her.

"I don't even have to be in your house. You forced me to come over, remember?"

"Well, if you feel that way, you can get the hell out. You get on my nerves, Nova. Always have to ruin a good day." I could hear her choke on her words.

I stood in the middle and watched the cat fight continue. That's how it was with these two. They never got along, ever since I could remember. And I could never understand why. I felt like Nova was ashamed of our mother. She worked as a lunch lady at a local high school, never had a husband, had two kids by two different men, and was always on some type of public assistance.

Nova wanted the good life. She wanted perfection: a wealthy husband, children, a nice house, car, and career. And she had it all except for the children.

"Calm down, you two. Nova, how was your day?" I attempted to deflect from the argument.

"It was fine. Thank you for asking. How was yours? Did you find out what you're going to do about tuition?"

I shook my head in shame. Ever since Nova found out that I lost my scholarship, she has been on my case. I appreciate that she's hard on me but sometimes I needed her to chill.

"You're shaking your head no? Girl, school starts in a month! Don't tell me you aren't going back. You came this far, you have to finish..."

"Leave her alone, damn it," My mother interrupted.

I wish neither of them ever knew about my school issues.

"I'll give you the tuition money," my mother said.

"How are you going to do that, Toni? You are broke your damn self unless you made us come over here so that you can tell us that you came into some mystery money," Nova fussed.

Nova called her mother by her name when she was upset with her, which was often.

Ignoring my sister, Ma replied, "I can take it out of the house, a second mortgage. They made me supervisor at the school, and I'm making more money now. I can afford to do this for you."

My sister rolled her eyes and sucked her teeth at my mother's offer.

"Mommy, I don't want you to go broke trying to help me fix this mess I made," I protested.

"She won't go broke. I will. Because when she can't afford to pay it back, she'll be hitting me up for the cash. I can help you with your books and some of your tuition and co-sign a student loan for you. We don't need Toni losing this house that's damn near paid for," Nova interjected, making me and my mother feel small.

She had a point. Whenever my mother was in a bind, Nova was there to help her out. I couldn't wait to be in a position to help my mother out.

"No thank you, Nova. I can handle this. I don't need your money. Listen, Skye, I got you. Full tuition for this year and no student loans. Okay baby?" my mother assured me while simultaneously rattling Nova's nerves.

She walked away, leaving my mother and I in the living room alone to talk in detail about the tuition.

***

Nova

Toni always does this shit! She bites off more than she can handle and leaves me to pick up the broken pieces. It gets on my nerves. I didn't work this hard to make this kind of money to throw it away. She is too old to be making these bad decisions.

Reaching in my crocodile Celine bag, I phoned my husband, who didn't answer. I then texted him to see where he was.

Me: Babe, where are you. My mother is driving me crazy.

Tyriq: Still at the office. Things are crazy. I should be there soon.

Sighing, I slipped my phone back into my bag. I was never the one to get in the way of his job. That takes priority over whatever surprise my mother had. Annoyed, I wandered back in the living room to find Skye and Toni sitting on the couch talking.

Just as I approached the sofa, the doorbell rang.

"Nova, please get that for me," Toni requested.

I moved towards the door and opened to find an older tall, stocky man standing on the other side. He looked familiar, but I couldn't place where I had seen him. His skin was the color of burnt sugar, and he had a full gray beard but a shiny, bald head.

"Hi sweetheart. You must be Nova." The stranger reached in for a hug. But I don't allow just anyone to touch me.

Backing up, I extended my arm and shook my head.

"Who are you?"

"Oh, you don't recognize me?" he cockily asked.

"Nope," I responded.

"I'm Rico Barnes. I used to play for the Redskins. You may recognize me from a few car dealership commercials."

"Hey baby," Toni interrupted before jumping off the couch and charging towards him.

"You have to forgive my daughter, she's had a stressful day," she continued, shooting me the evil eye before returning a loving gaze back to him.

I guess it's safe to assume that this was her new man. Not bad. He was definitely an upgrade from the losers she's dated in the past. Even though he was old, he was attractive. I just hoped he had some money.

"Sorry, if I came off rude. But yeah, I am Nova," I shook his hand. I was still guarded. When I turned around, Skye had joined the group.

"Hi, I'm Skye." She reached in for a hug. I rolled my eyes. She's always so trusting and open. And it always comes back to bite her in the ass. Just like it did with that little nigga she was messing with that tanked her grades.

"You haven't told them, have you?" he asked Toni, staring into her eyes.

"No! I'm waiting on you and your children."

"Just my oldest son and daughter will be coming." He smiled as he walked into the living room.

Before they could get seated comfortably, the doorbell rang again. This time Toni answered it. I'm assuming these were Rico's children. There was a young man and woman who both looked like him. They appeared to be in their late 20's – early 30's.

"Hey Sasha and Jr.," he greeted, ushering them into the room.

"Are we waiting for anyone else?" Rico continued while I looked at everyone suspiciously.

"Yep! You were waiting on me." The door opened and in walked Tyriq, dressed in a navy blue Armani suit, looking every bit of delicious. His deep cocoa was as smooth as velvet and it turned me on just to see him walk in a room.

"Hi baby!" My face lit up as I rushed to him and threw my arms around his neck.

He planted a sensual kiss to my cheek before walking towards the group of people gathered in Toni's living room.

After everyone made their introductions, we all settled down around my mother and Rico. Half the room seemed excited while the other half looked concerned.

Sasha and Jr.'s faces were set in frowns as they looked at our parents. My face matched theirs while Skye looked giddy right along with Toni and Rico.

"So, we gathered you all here today to make a very important announcement," Toni started.

"Yes, I've asked you ladies' mother for her hand in marriage. She said yes and..."

"We're getting married!" My mother finished his sentence.

"Oh my gosh! Congratulations!" My naïve sister jumped for joy. She threw her arms around our mother while I sat there with a raised eyebrow.

"I didn't know you were dating. How do you even know this man?" I snapped, bringing everyone back to reality.

As far as I knew, my mother was single and wasn't dating. Now, all of a sudden...

"Yeah, what the fuck, Pops?! Our mom has been dead, what? All of one month and now you're ready to marry this woman. How long have you known her?" Jr. rightfully questioned.

My husband's face was stunned. And Skye looked hurt at Jr.'s criticisms.

"Now son, keep it cool. No need to insult her."

"He didn't insult her. That was a legitimate question. Why are we just finding out about this relationship?" I pried.

"Chill out, Nova." My husband slipped his hand to my thigh, squeezing it. He hated when I got testy with my mother. And because I respected him, I shut my mouth. I could always talk to her later.

"Are you going to answer Jr.? Because it seems to me that you all probably have been carrying on for a while. Our mother died a month ago from a heart attack. She had been stressed out and depressed the last six months. Her hair was falling out, she was having panic attacks and couldn't sleep. But now it all makes sense. You were probably seeing this bitch behind her back and she knew about it!" Sasha lashed out. She stood up from the couch, ready to punch my mother.

I sat there, frozen in place.

"Bitch, you need to calm down and get the fuck out of our house. You're not going to come up in here calling my mother names!" Skye's sweet demeanor faded into ruthlessness.

"Ladies, ladies, everyone just needs to chill. Skye and Nova, go into the kitchen for a moment." My husband attempted to defuse the situation.

"Nah, they don't have to leave. We will. Come on, Sasha." The siblings rushed towards the door.

"Sasha and Jr., come back here! Don't you disrespect me or my new wife like this!" Rico hollered after them. But he might as well not been talking, because they kept walking and jumped in their cars.

"Is it true?" My lips finally parted while I sat there in a state of aggravation and amazement.

"No! How dare you ask me something like that? I met this wonderful man not too long ago and we fell in love." I could tell that she was lying.

I shook my head and gathered my bag.

"Let's go, Tyriq," I urged, leaving my mother and her new fiancé behind. There was no way in hell I could sit there in support of that foolishness. I was partial to his kids' accusation. My mother has always had an air of desperation with men.

"I'm sorry Ms. Johnson, congratulations. Peace, Skye," my husband replied before walking out with me.

"Nova, don't be like this!" Skye yelled as we exited.

I threw up my hand and waved. I had no time for that bullshit.

"Let her go! She ain't never been happy for me," Toni spat to Skye.

When we got outside my husband walked me to my car and placed his strong hands on my hips.

"Bae, what was that about?"

After all this time, his touch still made me melt. I bit my bottom lip and looked down before I responded. I hated for him to see me act bitchy.

"You know how my mother is. She's always doing impulsive shit like this. I can't support an engagement to a man I only met today. And besides, what if his kids were right?"

"So what. That's your mother. She needs your support and respect. You don't need to be treating her like this."

"Ugh, let me just go home and cool off. I'll see you there?"

"Later, I actually forgot to handle something in the office. Go home, take a bath, and then call your mother and apologize," he instructed.

"I'll try. And why can't you come home. Can't that office stuff wait until the morning?" I whined.

"You know it can't, babe. If I want this promotion by the end of the year, I have to be ahead of the game." His thumb trailed my chin before he planted his lips to mine.

He knew how to shut me up. And I rarely put up a fight.

"Okay, I'll see you later." I hugged him goodbye before jumping in my car and heading home, alone. I loved that he was a hardworking man, but sometimes I wished he would put my needs first.

Chapter 6

Tyriq

That drama at Toni's house left me stressed the fuck out. And I knew if I went home with my wife, she was going to talk about it all night long. I wasn't in the mood for that shit.

Hearing women bicker is akin to hearing nails on a chalkboard. It's excruciatingly obnoxious.

Instead of heading home to my wife, I hit up Kinasha to see if she wanted some dick tonight. Reaching into my glove compartment, I retrieved my secret burner phone which I kept to call my side chicks.

That bitch must have been waiting for my call because she answered after one ring.

"Hi daddy," she said in her cutesy, yet seductive voice. My dick was already at attention.

"What you doing?"

"Thinking about you. Why are you calling me so late? They wifey ain't around?" she pried.

"Don't worry about that. I'm coming over and you better be home waiting on me." I adjusted myself, while starting my car.

"I'm at the bar with my friend right now."

"I don't give a fuck. Take yo ass home. And when I get there you better already have been in the shower and wearing something sexy. Or nothing at all," I commanded.

"Yes, daddy. I'm leaving right now."

"Good girl. See you in 30." I hung up before sliding my phone back in the compartment before pulling off.

I loved that I had my women in check. I sent the wifey home as well as my side bitch, all within five minutes.

However, when I looked in the rearview mirror, I could see Ms. Toni staring at me while standing on her stoop, puffing a cigarette. Fuck! I hope she didn't catch me on the secret phone. I waved goodbye and she smiled and waved with her fingers. It almost looked seductive but it could be my crazy imagination. Since all I have is pussy on my mind.

***

I drove away from Toni's house on the south side of PG County to Kinasha's apartment in uptown DC. The only thing on my mind was busting it open and watching her suck me dry.

That's the thing, Nova rarely gave me head. She said it was something that should be reserved for special occasions. Thus, I only got it from her on my birthday and our anniversary. And when she did do it, it was wack.

Kinasha, on the other hand, was a pro.

When I got to her apartment, I buzzed her number but I got no answer. It pissed me the fuck off, because I told her to be ready. I don't have time to play around and wait for her.

Even though I lied to my wife about where I had to be, I still had to be home at a reasonable time.

Irritated, I dialed her number and she answered while giggling and talking to her friend.

"Where the fuck are you?"

"I'm pulling up right now. I didn't drive. I had to wait until my girl was ready to go."

"I don't care about your excuses. I gave implicit instructions," I barked.

"I'm sorry, daddy. I promise to make it up to you," she cooed in my ear.

"Damn right you will."

Agitated, I hung up and slid my phone back in my pocket.

In a few short seconds, she came racing to the apartment door.

"I'm so sorry."

"Damn right you are. Got me out here standing on your doorstep like a simp."

She kept saying sorry while quickly unlocking the front door before guiding me upstairs.

As soon as we got into her apartment, I grabbed her and wrapped my fingers around her precious neck. She moaned because she loved it when I got rough.

Pushing her into the wall, I glared into her eyes before speaking.

"I'm sorry," she whispered. I squeezed her neck even harder while rubbing my thumb along her skin.

"I told you to be ready for me. Now I have to punish you," I growled. She trembled underneath my touch.

"Punish me, daddy," she whispered. My hand wrapped even tighter around her neck while my free hand reached up her green dress.

There was no barrier between my hand and her pussy.

"Where the fuck are your panties? Who are you showing my pussy to?"

"Nobody baby. I just felt like being free," she moaned as I slipped two of my fingers in her tight slit.

After the months of pounding that coochie took from my dick, it was still snug, like a too small glove.

"You wanna be free?" I asked, while easing my fingers deeper inside her, eventually reaching her g-spot.

"Uh huh." She could barely speak.

"You not free tho. You my bitch. Don't ever let me catch you without panties unless it's in my office. You got that?"

"Yes baby," she whimpered. Her eyes rolled into the back of her head as if she was going to come and I was only fingering her.

She wasn't going to bust that easily. Swiftly, I slid my fingers out of her, causing her to exhale out loud.

I slipped my wet fingers to her mouth and she willingly sucked them.

"That's right, taste that shit. Taste your pussy." I lightly chuckled, while my hand was still around her neck.

Once I took my hand out of her mouth, I also released my hand from around her neck.

She looked up at me sheepishly, unsure of what to do next. I didn't give her too much time. I placed my hand to her head and pushed her down, forcing her to her knees.

"I miss sucking your dick, baby," she whispered as she undid my belt buckle and pants.

"Then suck it. Hurry up."

My pants dropped to the floor and she whipped all ten inches out. Wasting no time, she tongued my balls, immediately sending my eyes to the back of my head.

I love my wife, but if she don't learn to suck on my balls, I may never stop messing with other women.

Kinasha's tongue slipped around my sack before she made them disappear in her mouth. No matter how many times she has done it, I always watch in amazement. I looked down at her but her eyes were closed. She moaned as if she were the one receiving oral sex.

Still with her eyes shut, she slipped my balls out her mouth and trailed her tongue around the tip of my dick. Tasting my pre-cum, she moaned again.

"Open your eyes and look at me," I demanded. Doing as she was told, she locked eyes with mine and began wildly licking around the tip of my dick. Before I knew it, she slid my entire rod in her mouth.

Bobbing her head up and down, she slobbered all over me, making my black dick glisten. The best part was that she remained staring at me.

"That's right baby, suck that dick," I whispered before placing my hand to the back of her head.

Assisting her, I pushed her head down on my dick. The deeper I went into her throat the wetter her mouth became.

A lone tear trickled down her eye as she worked her mouth around me.

"Make me cum," I ordered. And what came next, I was not ready for. While my dick was in her mouth, she managed to also lick my balls. After about 30 seconds of that, I busted down her throat, the biggest nut. And like a pro, she swallowed every single drop.

Even licked the tip for any residual cum after she was done.

"Are you still mad at me?" she asked with a puppy dog look in her eyes while standing on her knees.

"Yep. Get up," I said, despite my knees wobbling. I felt as if they were going to buckle and I was going to fall to the ground. But I held my composure.

Following my commands, she stood up from the ground and pulled my hand to bring me in her bedroom.

When we got there, I ripped her dress off of her. It tore down the back but I didn't give a fuck.

"My dress!" she cried.

"Fuck that shit. If you were naked like I told you to be, then it wouldn't have gotten torn," I replied.

Despite wearing no panties, she was wearing a lacy pink bra. I unclasped it and threw it to the ground before lifting her up and tossing her little ass on the bed.

I turned her over and forced her on her hands and knees.

"Lick my pussy," she whispered.

"Nah, you on punishment," I responded.

Instead of acknowledging her request, I anchored myself behind her, staring at that pink treasure.

She was glistening and it was easy to see that she was ready to take this dick. I lifted it to her and began to massage her clit with my tip. She moaned and clutched at the sheets.

Rather than prolong the tease, I slipped my dick in her tight cunt.

"Oh shit!" she cried, but I remained focused.

My eyes were glued to the magnificent sight of seeing her teeny pussy conform to my girth. That shit was like magic.

I watched as her walls clenched me as I slowly moved out, making her even wetter with every stroke.

"Yes, baby," she moaned as she arched her little ass even more. I grabbed a hold of her long hair and wrapped it around my fingers while slamming into her. Her grip was stronger than a pit bull's jaw.

"I'm about to cum!" she shrieked as she erupted on my dick while burying her face into the mattress. Her fingers gripped the sheets but I didn't slow down.

I marveled at the frosting she left on me as I plunged in and out of her. Unable to take any more of my strokes, she brought her hand to my thighs, trying to push me away. But I wasn't having it.

"Where you think you going?" I asked while grabbing her hands behind her back. She screamed my name and bit at the sheets while I continued to stroke her. Before I knew it, I felt the urge to cum. Quickly, I pulled my rod out of her and said, "Suck it."

Kinasha turned around and devoured me once again while I gushed into the back of her throat. Like a ravenous beast, she swallowed and sucked every drop once again. My toes curled in ecstasy as my eyes rolled into the back of my head.

Finally she came up for air and laid back down on the bed, gazing up at me. I tumbled beside her, closing my eyes for a moment, making sure I didn't fall asleep.

"Why don't you stay the night?" she cooed as she trailed her fingers over my chest.

That was my cue to get the hell up.

"I can't. I gotta go." I jumped out of the bed and reached for my clothes and phone. When I checked the time, it was well after midnight. I knew that Nova would be knocked out and too tired to talk about her mother. I would be able to sneak in and take a shower before slipping into bed.

"Why do you always do that? Why can't you ever spend real time with me?" Kinasha's voice interrupted my thoughts of scheming.

"Don't start this shit again. I came over even though I told you I had somewhere else to be. If you wanna stop doing this, fine. We can stop but my situation isn't going to change," I spat while pulling my pants up.

"Fuck you Ty!" she screamed at me.

"Peace." I shrugged her off before gathering my things and jetting out the door.

She does this every single time, but tomorrow morning, she'll be acting like my best friend again.

Chapter 7

Nova

The past few days had been a blur. Tyriq had been working late to secure his impending promotion. And I've been ducking my mother's phone calls. The fact that she was getting married to a man she barely knew irritated me to no end. This woman was the queen of making terrible decisions.

Today I was spending my Saturday shopping with Misa before I met up with my husband for dinner. Together we rode to Pentagon City in my champagne colored Lexus. While we traveled there, I told her all about my mother's situation with her new fiancé.

"That is ridiculous, Nova!" She shook her head as I pulled into the parking lot.

"I know, girl. His kids were there, accusing them of sleeping around behind their mother's back. It was a mess. And now she's blowing up my phone."

I backed into the space and turned the ignition off.

"But enough of that. What's going on with you and Xavier?"

"I called that little bitch. She was so damn rude. Nova, I just can't believe Xavier would put me through this." Misa began to choke on her words as tears filled her eyes.

"I already told you, leave him. It's not worth the headache."

"And I already told you, I cannot do that. He is the one with the money. And I can't raise these children without him. I just need him to stop seeing that hoe!"

"Have your brother take care of it," I suggested, with a sinister grin.

Her brother was a kingpin named Chop, and he could handle getting rid of a little bitch. Especially a bitch getting in the way of his sister's happiness.

"I can't have Chop kill my husband. That would be too messy, since my brother is an ADA," she protested.

However, she missed what I was saying.

"No, he shouldn't kill Xavier. He should get rid of the girl."

I know that seems fucked up, that I would suggest that a thot should die. But these bitches needed to learn. They can't just ruin people's families and get away with it. They're so worthless. Those hoes scar children, suck money from men, and wreak havoc in everyone's lives.

One less hoe in the streets could save many families. That bitch has to go.

"You might be onto something. I'll def speak with Chop."

We exited the car and headed into the mall. As we drifted in and out of stores, we each picked up some cute clothes. I bought a sexy lacy black dress from BCBG and a pair of taupe Alexander McQueen heels for my dinner with Tyriq.

Misa bought a few pairs of jeans and something for the kids. As we stepped into the MAC store I received another phone call from my mother. Fed up with her blowing my phone up, I finally decided to answer.

"Yes Toni," I sighed.

"Look who finally decided to answer." Her sarcasm grated my nerves.

"What do you want Toni?" I asked.

"I am your mother! Show me some damned respect," she snarled.

"I'll show you some damned respect when you show yourself some respect. How are you going to get engaged to a man you barely know? And right after his wife died?!"

"For your information, we are officially married now. We eloped yesterday. Skye went with us as a witness since you and his children were acting stubborn. We decided to go get married at the courthouse. I was just calling you to let you know."

I was too tired of my mother's antics to care. Instead, I was more upset that my sister didn't say anything to me.

"Congratu-fuckin'-lations," I replied before hanging up and returning back to the MAC counter.

"Who was that?" Misa asked as she tried on different shades of purple lipstick.

"My mother. She and that rusty football player got married."

"She wasted no time!"

"And that's what the problem is," I surmised, turning back to the make-up brushes, blushes, and eye shadows.

***

When I got home after shopping with Misa, my intentions were to hop in the shower and start on my make-up for my dinner out with Tyriq. He still wasn't home yet from getting work done in the office. My man was so dedicated to his job that he went in on many Saturdays so that he could be ahead.

Dropping my bags near the stairs, I looked around at the place I was blessed to call mine. Our modern furniture from West Elm was sleek, not scuffed, and was without stains. All DVDs and books were standing perfectly on their shelves. And our white carpet was free of blemishes. Our home was perfectly neat, the benefits of not having children.

Even though I enjoyed the luxury of coming into a well put together place, I would trade it in for a few children running around. But I know that my husband wants to wait. So, I'll be patient, waiting for the day that he makes me a mother.

Fresh out the shower in my terry cloth robe, I cleared the foggy mirror so that I could begin working on my face. As I applied moisturizer, I heard the alarm beep. Tyriq was home. My belly fluttered as if a thousand butterflies had taken space there.

Years into our union and he still excited me as if I were a teenage girl with a persistent crush. I closed the door to the bathroom to shield my beauty regimen. Despite us being married, he never saw what it took me to become beautiful. I never allowed him to see my entire routine.

That's where bitches mess up. They get too comfortable with their men. There's no mystery and once that's gone, he treats you like he's used to you. And that's when his eye begins to wander to something new. Something mysterious. At least that's how it's been in my past.

Every boyfriend I had before Tyriq cheated on me. And I was determined to keep Tyriq from cheating on me. I tried to be the most perfect wife for him. And in return, he adores me. And hasn't cheated on me.

Once I finished applying my make-up and fixing my hair, I opened the bathroom door, still dressed in my robe. Tyriq was standing in the room, glancing down at his cell phone, with a frustrated look on his face.

"Show me what's under that robe." He grinned when he looked up from the phone.

"Don't we have a reservation?" I bit down on my bottom lip.

"Yeah, but I'm starving for you."
His strong hands reached into my robe and landed on my ass. He squeezed me as he brought his lips to my neck and began to suckle me, causing my knees to grow weak. I could feel them buckling under the touch of his tongue to my flesh.

Slowly, he knelt down and dropped my robe around my ankles. Reaching from behind, he grabbed my ass and planted his face between my thighs before lifting me up and carrying me to the bathroom.

I loved how strong he was. All of those hours in the gym paid off. He was able to lift me up on his shoulders and carry me all over this damn house.

When we got into the bathroom, he planted me down on the counter with my legs stretched apart. Feverishly, his tongue whipped around my clit, causing me to tremble. My heart pounded against my sternum while I clutched onto the sink with one hand and his back with the other.

He was still wearing a crisp white shirt from when he went into the office. My manicured nails dug into his shirt as the sensations spread throughout my body like an uncontrollable wildfire.

I had no control over anything as he held me close to his face. My body was burning with passion and not even the cold sink pressed to my ass could cool me down.

With my smooth brown legs draped over his shoulder, he slid his index and middle finger into my love tunnel and began to toy with my g-spot. Unable to take it anymore, I banged my head against the mirror and began to squirt all over his face. He sopped me up like I was a melting sundae that he didn't want to waste.

My heart exploded out of my chest as my breath rapidly escaped me. Vision blurry, skin tingly, I slumped against the mirror as he came up.

Laughing, he reached for a towel and cleaned his face.

"Our reservation is at 8:00. Let me hop in the shower really quickly," he finally said as I slid from off the sink.

While he was in the shower, I cleaned myself up and got dressed. I slid into the lacy black dress that made my cleavage pop and my waist appear tiny. The stilettos made my calf muscles look amazing and I knew that when my husband got out of the shower, his jaw was going to drop. Hell, he may not have wanted to even go anywhere.

Once out of the shower, he got dressed in a navy sport coat, a pale blue button up, and a pair of black slacks. The diamond cufflinks in his wrists were blinding, matching the studs that pierced his ears. He looked scrumptious enough to devour. But I held my composure, because I was hungry as hell. I hadn't eaten anything since my tryst at the mall with Mia.

"I got something for you," he announced before stepping behind me. I could hear the opening of a jewelry case.

"What did you get me?" My face lit up with joy. He was always surprisingly me with things. Last week it was a tennis bracelet. The week before that, it was a real python bag.

"Shhhh..." he responded, while draping a cold necklace around my neck. With precision, he fastened the clasps.

My curious fingers reached for the new piece of jewelry, gliding over what felt like diamonds.

"Go look at yourself in the mirror," he encouraged with a hint of cockiness steeped in his voice. Whatever was around my collar must have been luxurious.

And when I looked at my reflection, my presumptions were confirmed. It was the diamond necklace he saw me lust over in the Miami Harry Winston. We vacationed in South Beach about a month ago. One day while strolling down the street, this spectacular piece of jewelry caught my eye. However, when I saw the price was $50,000, I quickly turned my attention away.

"How can you afford this?" I gasped while gushing over the brilliance of the diamonds.

"Don't ask me no shit like that. It's yours, I got it," he snapped, forcing me to immediately feel bad for questioning him.

"I'm sorry, you're right. And I do love it. Its beautiful."

"You deserve it, baby." He planted a kiss on my cheek, making me feel warm all over.

This was going to be a good night.

Chapter 8

Tyriq

When we arrived at Sax, a French restaurant in downtown D.C., I paid for a valet. My wife looked gorgeous tonight, as always. Her silky skin glinted underneath the moonlight and it took everything in me to not cancel the reservation and take her ass back in the house.

I wanted to taste her pussy again. Yeah, I know I cheat on her, but I never eat another hoe's pussy. There are some things I reserve for my wife.

Placing my hand at her lower back, we entered the restaurant, where the hostess guided us to a balcony table overlooking the entire place. It had been a few weeks since we had a real date since I had been so caught up with work. I really was trying to secure this promotion.

"What are you thinking about getting?" she asked me while her eyes scanned the decadent menu.

"Surf and turf. That Kobe beef with lobster sounds delicious." My stomach growled at the description of the dish. I didn't even wince when I saw the price of $145. Fuck it, sometimes you have to treat yourself.

"What about you?" I asked her in return.

"The salmon or the scallops. I can't decide." Her eyes never lifted off of the menu.

"Get both," I suggested.

Her eyes lifted from the menu and stared at mine as if to say, are you serious?

"Get both. Eat a little bit of them each and take the rest home. You shouldn't have to only pick one. Get whatever you like." I tried to treat my lady to whatever she wanted. It was my goal to ensure that she never wanted for anything. No matter what it took.

When I saw her eyes light up over that necklace in Harry Winston, I knew I had to get it for her. It was well out of my price range. But when there's a will, there is a way. I finagled with the finances at my job and borrowed some money to get her the necklace. I have a huge contract at the end of the month; if it all goes well then I will be able to put the money back before anyone notices. I'm 99% sure the contract is going through, so I'm not worried.

After we sat there talking, our waitress approached us. And when I looked up to see who it was, my stomach knotted. I swear I even almost swallowed my tongue. My waitress was Kinasha.

"Hey Mr. and Mrs. Shelton," she greeted with a glare of mischief in her eye. She always called me by my last name in front of my wife and other coworkers. But what in the fuck was she doing here?

"Oh hey, Kinasha. How long have you been working here?" My naïve wife asked Kinasha, who looked at us both as if she were about to spill the beans.

I prayed that she didn't say anything, but even if she did, I would deny that shit and have her fired.

"I need a new car, and you know Durden doesn't pay me nearly enough." She rolled her eyes at me before refocusing her attention on my wife.

"That's terrible. My husband tells me you're a wonderful assistant. Babe, she's been with you for two years, you can't request to get her a raise?" I wanted to tell my wife to shut the fuck up.

The truth of the matter is, she's a shitty assistant. She takes lengthy lunch breaks, talks on her phone, eats at her desk, and is occasionally rude to visitors. The office wants me to fire her, but instead I've told them she is on probation. If she fucks up again, she will be fired. But I fear she will snitch about our union, which is why I try to leave no evidence of us fucking.

"Yeah, Mr. Shelton, can you speak up for me and get me a raise? You know how much work I put in. I do what I do really good too," she slickly added. She was playing games right now, and if she kept up, I was going to toss her little ass over the balcony.

"Stop by my office first thing in the morning, and we can talk about it," I spat between gritted teeth.

She giggled before taking our orders. In addition to the food, I made sure to add a bottle of champagne. It was going to be a long ass night and I didn't trust her not to spit in our food. But if I was tipsy, I wouldn't be able to think about it.

While we waited for our dinner to arrive, Nova began to talk to me about her mother, further driving me to drink.

"And she and that nigga got married!" she exclaimed across from me. I picked up a bottle of the bubbly and poured me another glass before tossing it down my throat.

"Slow down, you have to drive," she nagged. "I can't believe she did that. She doesn't know him. I feel like he is just going to use her..." Nova continued. Her voice was beginning to aggravate me. But it wasn't really her. It was the fact that Kinasha was in here serving us.

The pressure became almost too much to bear. Before I knew it I said in between clenched teeth, "Shut the hell up about your hoe ass mother."

"Are you kidding me? What the fuck is your problem?" Nova appeared startled. It even shocked me that I had spoken to her that way. Out the corner of my eye I could see Kinasha staring at us.

"I'm tired of hearing about your mother. All you do is complain about her sometimes. Let that shit go." I finished off another glass of champagne, which concluded the whole bottle.

In a flash, Kinasha was at our side.

"Would you all like another bottle? You sure finished that fast." She giggled.

"Yes, please," Nova answered without tearing her eyes away from me. Kinasha walked away with a pep in her step as if she knew that my wife and I were arguing.

The stress of her waiting on us was wearing me out. I wanted to leave but I didn't want to ruin this night even more than I already did.

"What is your problem? If I can't come to you, my own husband, about my family shit, who can I come to? I need someone to listen to me. Not someone who shuts me down every time I try to talk about my feelings."

But before I could reply, a busboy brought our food. Although I was too stressed to eat it, I stuck my knife and fork in the lobster, hoping Nova would do the same.

Instead, she just stared at me with disbelief in her eyes.

"You're really blocking me out? You're just going to sit up here and eat and not respond to me."

"Damn Nova, a nigga can't even enjoy his meal with you out here nagging. This steak is 150 bucks. All I want to do is enjoy it, shit. But no, you want to come in here complaining about your mother. I got you that necklace you wanted. Took you out. Ate your pussy. Now you want to fight?!" I flipped on her.

I was still keeping my voice low so that no one could hear me. But the truth is, I was ready to leave. I no longer wanted to be here. And while I wasn't truly mad at my wife, she added fuel to the fire. I was really pissed at Kinasha.

When that little bitch saw that she was waitress, she could have asked for another table, given me a head nod, and kept it moving.

"You know what Ty, fuck you. I'm leaving," she said before lifting away from the chair. She grabbed her purse and darted past Kinasha and another busboy before marching down the stairs.

Kinasha quickly walked over as I stood from the table so that I could catch up with my wife.

"Trouble in paradise?" she instigated.

"Bitch, you know damn well what you're doing." I shook my head while peeling off a few hundreds.

"It's not my fault that you all don't pay me enough and I have to work here. It ain't my fault that she doesn't make you happy. I see you stressed out. Come by after I get off of work."

"Get the fuck out of my face," I replied, leaving a wad of cash on the table.

"Fine, be like that, baby. But I will be in your office on Monday inquiring about my raise," she giggled as I waved her off and headed downstairs.

When I got there, Nova was nowhere in sight. I tried calling her several times but it just went straight to voicemail. The valet brought my car back around and I circled the block looking for her.

I guess she must've gone home.

Chapter 9

Skye

I squeezed my body into a pair of high waist acid wash jeans and a light pink crop top. Aoki told me she would be over my house in twenty minutes to take me to a lounge with her, so I had to get cute. I did my make-up to look soft, yet sexy. Complete with bronzer, a smoky eye, and a pink matte lip, I looked ready for the nightlife.

Instead of putting on my shoes, I decided to wait until she got here. There was no use in hurting my feet before I even got a chance to get into the lounge.

As I walked past my refrigerator, I noticed my calendar. Then it hit me like a ton of bricks. My tuition was due in one week. And school started in two.

Since my mother had gotten married, I had been trying not to stress her out about my tuition. I wanted to give her time to enjoy her new husband. But I needed to get this money so that I could graduate.

Reaching for my phone, I dialed her number and she answered after a few rings.

"Hi my favorite daughter," she giggled in my ear.

"You don't mean that. You love Nova and I just the same," I protested. Apparently, she and Nova had another fight over the last few days. That's how it always is with them. Cats and dogs. They can never seem to get along

"But she doesn't love me like you do."

"Ma, stop it. I called to see if you had gotten the money for my tuition. I need to pay it ASAP," I spoke firmly, while applying the final touches to my make-up.

"Oh shit, Skye. I forgot to tell you."

My heart began to race. I hoped that she wasn't reneging, because if she were, I was fucked.

"Forgot to tell me what?" I asked, dropping my mascara on the counter.

"I let Rico borrow the money so that he can open up his new business. He's opening a car wash, baby. And as soon as the profits start rolling in, he's going to pay me back double! Then I will pay your tuition."

"Ma, how could you! I can't wait until his business opens. I start school in two damn weeks!" I shouted. I could hear her grow silent. She had never heard me curse before since I tried to remain respectful. Growing up, I saw how Nova reacted towards her, so I strived to be different. But today she was plucking my nerves.

"Watch your mouth, Skye, I am still your mother."

"Then act like it! How the hell are you going to put him before me? Don't you know this is my senior year?!" I shrieked as someone knocked on my door.

Knowing that it was Aoki, I quickly opened it up and in she walked, sipping a blue Slurpee. This bitch was too grown to be drinking blue shit. Her tongue and mouth matched the frozen drink.

"Skye, you are a smart girl. You made it this far without the money. I'm sure you can figure this out. Perhaps you can take out a loan."

"A loan! I don't even have any credit. And you have not contributed nothing to my education since I been in school. You owe me this!" I couldn't believe what I was hearing.

Tears began to sting my eyes, as my palms grew sweaty. I couldn't believe she was putting me in this position.

"Look Skye, talk to that boujie sister of yours. She can help you. And as for a loan, it's temporary. I will pay it off as soon as Rico gives me my money," she reasoned. It was as if she didn't even hear what I was saying.

Sure, I could take out a loan. But it's the principle of it all. She lied to me!

"If you knew you weren't going to be able to give me the money, you should have kept quiet. You are always going back on your word!"

"It ain't my fault you got caught up with some dick last year and lost your scholarship. You went back on your word. You promised those people you would get good grades so you could keep that money, but you didn't. You let that nigga get your head twisted."

"Well, the apple doesn't fall far from the tree, now does it?" I retorted before ending the call.

When I looked up at Aoki, she was cracking the fuck up.

"Bitch, are you laughing at my serious situation!"

"Yes, hoe, I am." She continued to snicker.

"That's why you look like you been sucking on Smurf dicks!" I sassed before sliding my feet in my black open toe booties.

"But those Smurf dicks pay me!" She laughed even harder, which made me giggle as well.

"You are so disgusting," I thrashed, while shaking my head with a faint smile on my face.

"And you are pathetic. You out here begging your mother for tuition money. That bitch hasn't done shit for you since you graduated high school. You're the one that got yourself those scholarships, this apartment, and that busted ride you keep pushing around town. She's done nothing for you!"

I loved how Aoki could look at things from a realistic perspective. Sometimes I wished I wasn't as naïve. If I had more sense, I would have never gotten involved with Chad and lost my scholarship. And consequently, I would have never trusted my mother to do something she promised. But I couldn't help but be livid. For once in my life, I felt the hatred that Nova harbored for our mother. Honestly, the bitch was better off dead so that I could get the insurance money.

Lord forgive me for thinking such a horrible thought about my mother.

"You're right. I'm in such a tight spot right now. I don't make enough at the restaurant where I bartend to pay rent."

"Trick, I already knew that. That's why I been trying to put you on. You are a beautiful girl. And you're smart. There's a lot of niggas who would be willing to pay to spend time with you."

There she goes again with this hoe shit.

"I'm not selling ass. I respect my body too much."

"What's your plan then?" She cocked her head to the side while pursing her lips.

"Take out a loan and wait until she can pay me back."

"You know damn well that's never going to happen. Your mother ain't the type to marry a smart nigga. That nigga is going to take her money and not do a thing with it."

"Then I'll struggle paying back my loan. I'm not selling my ass like you. I believe in love and commitment."

"That's okay. You can believe in love and commitment while a bitch like me will fuck whoever you love and is committed to," she clapped back.

Feeling sorry for her, I shook my head because she truly believed that shit.

"Are you ready?" she asked.

"Yep," I replied before we stepped outside.

She walked ahead of me and I finally noticed the shoes she was sporting. They were a pair of Jimmy

Choos. With all the money she got men to spend on shoes, she could have had her degree too. Then it got me to thinking, maybe I could get at least one sugar daddy to help me with tuition. Where's the harm in that?

"Why are you so quiet?" Aoki asked as we cruised towards U Street.

"I was thinking about what you said. I think you should show me the ropes."

"Finally, she sees the light!" She playfully raised her hand to the ceiling as she was sending up praise.

***

We ended up at Blue Smoke, a new hookah lounge off of U Street. When we walked through the front door, we handed our I.D.s to the bouncer. After that we sashayed to the bar, turning heads along the way.

"These niggas in here are feeling you," she whispered in my ear when we approached the bar. The blue color on her tongue had faded and she no longer looked like she been suckin' off blue men.

I giggled to myself at the ridiculous thought.

"So, how do you do it? Do you wait for them to come up to you? Or do you approach them?" I asked as she leaned into the bar.

"First of all, I don't look for them in places like this. Look around, all these niggas in here are broke! The dudes with figures are not found in hip hop hookah lounges. You have to go downtown or in affluent areas."

"So why did you drag me here? I thought you were on the prowl," I prodded. Earlier when she invited me out she said it was business related. And the only business she has is sleeping with married men.

"Remember that club I used to strip at?"

"You mean the one where you lasted no more than a month?"

"Yup, that one. The owner said he had a job for me to do. So I'm meeting him here. His name is Chop."

"Oh I see." I nodded as she ordered us two Coronas and shots of Cuervo.

"Turn up!" she shrilled, slamming her shot glass into mine before we both knocked the burning elixir back.

"Okay, CrazySexyCool, I'll be right back because I think I saw him walk in. By the way, he owns this spot too. Why don't you meet a dude and practice flirting at least," she instructed before switching away.

I felt awkward standing at the bar alone, so I ordered shisha, mango and mint flavor. The server brought it to me pretty quickly and I began to smoke to take my mind off of being alone.

"Where's your man?" A deep voice snuck into my ear from behind. Slowly, I turned around to see who it was. And when my eyes met his, my heart began to flutter.

The man standing before me had a pair of hazel eyes complemented by his butterscotch skin. The scent of his Tom Ford cologne wafted past my nostrils, sending me on a high.

"I came here with one of my girls." I finally mustered a reply.

"You won't be leaving with her." He stepped even closer, his height towering over me. It was rare that I had to look up at a man, considering I'm 5'10".

"I don't even know you. How dare you make that assumption." My face twisted in disgust, but my heart was racing. Whoever this man was, he was fine enough for me to leave with him.

He had a Caesar cut with deep waves. His beard was thick and had a healthy sheen. In his ears, he rocked a pair of diamonds that were definitely worth more than everything I had on.

"I'm Quantrell. But you can call me Quan. Now are you ready to leave?" He chuckled, exposing his perfectly straight white teeth. His smile rivaled the brightness of the diamonds in his ear.

"You are crazy. There is no way in hell I'm leaving with you." I shook my head while biting down on my lip.

"Ahhh, I get it now. You want me to know your name. And that is..."

"It's Skye," I replied.

"That's a sexy name. I peeped you when you and your girl walked in. You almost looked out of place." He licked his bottom lip.

"What makes you say that?"

"Before I answer that, you want something to drink?"

"Yeah, a Corona with lime, please."

"See, that's what I mean. You out of place. *Please*..." He mocked me in a whiny voice before ordering me a Corona and him a Heineken.

"You look too boujie to be in a spot like this. It's grimy in here."

"Then what are you doing here?"

"My nigga just opened this spot. So, I came to show him some love. But you, you look too soft and sweet to be in here. Your nigga need to be keeping you with him, for real."

"I'm single, thank you very much."

"Fuck that. You mine then." He laughed before bringing the bottle back to his mouth. My eyes lingered on his lips a little too long. Luckily, I broke my gaze away just as he returned his vision back to me.

"What do you do? Are you in school?" he probed while I swallowed some of my beer.

"Yeah, I go to GW for dance and education. I want to be a teacher when I graduate. And right now I'm a bartender at Fridays."

"Oh you a youngin'. How old are you?"

"I just turned twenty-one," I replied, embarrassed.

"How old are you?" I asked back.

"Thirty-five. Old enough to show you a few things," he spat, causing me to feel tingly inside. I could feel my pussy moisten at the thought of the things he could show me.

"You're crazy. I can't go there with you."

"Yeah, not tonight at least. I gotta make sure you ready for a real nigga. So, give me your number and I'll hit you up," he seduced me. There was something about him that set me aflame.

Typically, I gave niggas a hard ass time when they were trying to get my number. But today, I typed my number in his phone without any hesitation.

***

Aoki

Chop, my old boss, called earlier today because he said he had a job for me. Back when I was still in school with Skye, I was running coke for him and was even selling some on campus. However, I started with stripping in his club. But it became too much and I wanted out. I didn't want to strip nor run coke.

Of course, like a real goon, he wasn't having it. He thought I was being shady and was working on ratting him out. But that couldn't have been further from the truth. I was afraid of getting caught. After begging and pleading him, he told me I could quit running drugs, but I only if I still did a few jobs for him.

Every once in a while, he needs me to finesse a nigga, to get him in a compromising situation so that he could rob him.

But if my big brother was around to see what I was doing he would be livid! My brother Miyagi was sent to prison a few years ago and was then placed in witness protection. He was never able to tell us why, and now I can't even get in contact with him.

Chop believes that Miyagi is a snitch. He would say why else would they put him in witness protection? But I don't believe it. My brother lives and will die by the code. He doesn't talk to the feds. Never have, never will.

Him and Chop used to run together, but my brother was arrested on possession charges. They gave him twenty-five years, and the last I heard he was fighting it in appeals. Then he disappeared. He called one day and said he was going into witness protection and he would call me as soon as he can.

That was four years ago, my senior year of college. I pray daily that he's still alive. And I guess if he were to be die, they would let us know. But my mother and I still worry about him.

"What up!" Chop greeted when I entered his back office. The room was brightly lit compared to the rest of the smoky club. Under the fluorescent lights was a marble desk surrounded by security

88

monitors. He could see every single thing that happened in the club from what goes down behind the bar to the hallway where the bathrooms were.

"You tell me. You called me here," I sassed before plopping down on the leather couch in his office. I crossed my legs, exposing my sexy outer thighs, catching his attention.

"I need you to lay off Xavier," he flatly stated while rolling a joint of a Dutch.

"Why? And how do you even know about him?" My eyebrow rose to the ceiling. This nigga was messing with my bread. Xavier sponsored me very well even though he has a wife and three kids.

Chop licked around the paper, rolling it into the perfect blunt. He was a sexy nigga. 6'2", chocolate skin, long dreads that were always neat, and a pair of the sexiest lips I've ever seen on a man. I've lost count of how many times I've daydreamed about sitting on his face. But we've never fooled around because my brother would kill me if he found out.

"Don't question me. Just do it. Stop seeing him."

"And how am I supposed to pay my car lease?" It was a silly question because the truth is, I had enough money saved to live off of for about six months. But I like to keep stacking.

"Get a fucking job or you can run for me again." He laughed out loud.

"Nigga please. We both know that those aren't options."

"Lazy ass little girl. Your brother would be ashamed of you if he knew that you were out here doing."

"And he want to toe-tag you if he knew that you were paying me to do it sometimes. Now why else did you call me down here?"

"Leave Xavier alone and in exchange, I got another nigga I need you to finesse."

"Who?"

"This nigga named Tyriq. I can pay you to fuck with him for a while because I need some info. When the time comes, I'll let you know exactly what I need. But you can't mess with him and Xavier at the same time. If I find out that you still fucking him I will strangle your ass."

"You wouldn't lay a finger on me. My brother…"

"Where is your brother? Do you see him anywhere? No, I didn't think so. No one knows where that nigga is and if I body you, he won't realize it until he's released. And that's IF he is released." I knew not to play with Chop, but that nigga didn't have the heart to kill me. But I guess I shouldn't take any chances.

"I hope you know, I remember every time you threaten me. And WHEN my brother gets out I will be telling him. He will come down here and make sure you have a closed casket funeral. Don't fuck with me," I barked back at him. He didn't take me seriously. Instead, he erupted into laugher.

"You're so cute when you get mad. Awww. Little girl is mad at me? Get the fuck over it and do your damn job. I'm going to text you the deets on the nigga Tyriq. You'll be paid well for your services. Now get the fuck out of my office before you irritate me."

Shaking my head, I stood up from the comfort of the couch. His eyes followed my shapely legs as I pulled my mini-skirt down.

I turned and walked to the door. I know he was looking at my ass. A fat ass he will never get to touch.

"I expect a down payment by tomorrow morning. And then I will get to work," I said before walking out of the door.

When I got back into the main lounge area, I saw Skye giving her number to some sexy light-skinned nigga with light eyes. He looked much older than her, but he was definitely fine. I could see from here he wasn't wearing a wedding ring. This bitch doesn't follow directions.

I told her to only fuck with a nigga who is married because they are more grateful. They are trapped in their marriages and ain't getting no pussy. These single niggas get pussy like it's water.

"Wsup," I said when I approached her. The guy who was standing with her had left her side by now.

"Hey, how was that meeting?" she asked while smiling ear to ear. That nigga wrapped her up for about ten minutes and she already had her nostrils open.

"It was fine. But damn bitch, you look dictamized. Who was that?"

"His name is Quan. He's thirty-five and he's single."

"You don't listen! I said married niggas only. Maybe you can get away with an engaged nigga. At least tell me what he does? If he got bread, then you can rock with him."

I saw the excitement in her face fall.

"I don't know what he does."

"So, he could be a broke nigga. I thought you needed money."

"I do but I liked him. And you know I'm not cut out for this shit," she whined.

"Whatever, but when your ass can't pay tuition and you end up stripping in some club, don't say I didn't tell you so." I rolled my eyes before reaching for my phone. Someone was calling me and when I looked at my caller ID it was Xavier.

I hit ignore and sent him a text message that read: It's over nigga. Go be with your wife.

I giggled before sliding my phone back in my bag. These niggas get so attached.

I partied the rest of the night with Skye. Luckily, we were cute. Men bought our drinks the rest of the night. And Chop covered our hookah. I hope whoever this nigga he wants me to fuck with is fine though. That usually makes the job easy.

Chapter 10

Nova

The night Tyriq and I went out to dinner, he showed me a side of him I had never encountered. I had never heard him speak to me that way and be so disrespectful. That night, I bolted out of that restaurant and took an Uber home.

When he came back home that night, he apologized profusely and even took me on a shopping spree the next day. But clothes and shoes can't make up for the embarrassment I felt. He was trying to make it up to me, but it was taking me longer to forgive him than usual.

"Nova, what time are you going to lunch?" my coworker and friend Kiss asked. Yes, her mother named her Kiss.

"I have to finish up these press releases. I at least want to get the first drafts done before I eat. Your ass is always hungry," I playfully teased as she stepped closer into my office while closing the door behind her.

"That's because I'm pregnant," she said, her face lighting up with joy.

I didn't say anything. I just sat there staring at her like she had lost her mind. Just two months ago she was crying about her husband cheating on her with some young bitch. Now she was having his baby. Not only did that bother me, but the fact that these women with ain't shit husbands kept giving them babies, while my good husband didn't want any yet.

"Why are you making that face?" she asked me, her eyes filled with concern.

"He cheats on you. Are you sure you want to bring an innocent baby into that?"

"This will bring us closer. This will make him stay home," she foolishly reasoned.

Rather than tell her the millions of reasons why that was false, I offered her a forced smile and said, "Congratulations."

"Thank you! That's all I need from you, is to be happy for me."

"If you're happy, then I'm happy for you. Let's do lunch at 1:30. I should be finished by then," I suggested.

She smiled before exiting my office. As soon as the door closed behind her, I rolled my eyes. This simple bitch should know better. Then again, she is only twenty-four years old. But she'll see that he won't change after the baby is here. Cheating men never changed.

I continued to work on the press releases so that I could eat lunch with her. While I wasn't necessarily pressed to talk to her, I was starving.

"Can I speak with you a moment?" Andrea, my manager, asked when she knocked on my door.

"Sure, come in." I hit save on my documents and gave her my full attention.

Andrea was cool but I always had to be on my p's and q's around her. This woman determined whether I moved up in the company.

"I wanted to let you know, I pitched your name to lead this new campaign," she announced before sliding into the chair in front of my desk. She swiped her blonde hair behind her ear.

"What campaign?"

"It's for Durden Development. They are building some new condos and need help with rallying the community behind it. Many people are upset about *that ghetto* being destroyed. So, I pitched you as a PR manager."

The way she said that ghetto made my stomach twist. That ghetto is where many poor people call home. At one point, I called The Gardens home. We lived there for a chunk of my childhood until my mother got that house. So, it had a special place in my heart, no matter how I tried to deny my poor childhood.

"Thank you for pitching me."

"You're welcome. I'll give you more details as they come," she added before leaving my office.

A part of me felt uncomfortable with the project while another part of me was excited. Durden Development was the name of the company my husband worked at. In fact, I wanted to go see him on his lunch break, rather than eat with Kiss.

I jetted out of the office and texted Kiss to let her know I had to see my husband because of an emergency. Hopefully, he wasn't too busy to eat with me...

***

Tyriq

"Why won't you come over anymore? I already apologized for the way I acted when I saw you out with your wife..." Kinasha whined to me while I attempted to get work done.

My nose was buried in the pile of financials sitting on my desk and I had no time to deal with her shit.

"Go back to work. I'm busy," I said without looking up with her.

What happened over the weekend almost made me lose my wife and I wasn't trying to go back there.

"I'm sorry, Ty! I really am. I swear that shit won't happen again. Please don't be done with me, baby!" she pleaded but I still refused to look up at her. There was too much on the line.

Before I knew it, she turned away and locked my office door, which forced me to view her.

"What the fuck are you doing?" I asked.

"You seem tense, Ty, let me take care of you."

"Kinasha, I'm done with your ass. You don't know your motherfuckin' place. Nova is my wife and I am never going to leave her."

'That's fine. But let me relieve your stress while you're here at work." She bit down on her lip before unbuttoning her blouse, exposing her Victoria's Secret leopard bra.

My dick jumped at the visual of her perky tits protruding towards me.

"Put your shirt back on," I protested, but she ignored me. Instead, she walked over to me and dropped to her knees. My dick throbbed with anticipation.

"I'm serious, Kinasha, put your clothes back on and go back to work."

"I'm trying to put in work now. Let me work on you since you my boss," she whispered as her small hands crawled to my belt buckle.

Undoing my pants, she began to jerk me off while flicking her tongue around the tip. I relaxed in my chair. There was no point in fighting her. Besides, I haven't busted a nut in damn near a week since Nova was still upset with me.

I tilted my head back and my eyes rolled up in my head. While she bobbed up and down on my rod, I brought my hand to the back of her head, gently forcing her to deep throat me.

Just as I was beginning to get into it we heard someone pull at my doorknob.

"Shit," I mumbled as I pushed Kinasha away. She had a look of shock on her face as she scrambled to button up her shirt.

"Ty, are you in there?" I heard my wife call out from the other side of the door.

"What is your wife doing here?" Kinasha whispered.

I shrugged maniacally while pointing to the area underneath my desk. She needed to scoot her little ass there and hide.

In response to my ridiculous suggestion, she sucked her teeth until I shoved her towards the desk. Obeying me, she crawled underneath and scooted my office chair to meet her.

"Ty!"

"Coming babe," I shouted back as I zipped my pants up.

I opened the door and Nova walked right past me.

"What are you doing here?" I asked.

"I'll get to that in a second. Why was your door locked?" she questioned as she neared me. I stood in front of my desk and leaned against it, trying to act casual.

"I keep it locked because sometimes the cleaning ladies bust in and it disrupts my flow of work. I just got off of a conference call and didn't want any interruptions. Now what brings you here?" I attempted to flip the subject back to her.

"Where is your assistant?"

"She's at lunch."

"What does she even do around here? Every time I come here she is on her phone or at lunch."

"Weren't you the one who was saying she should ask for a raise when we saw her at dinner?" I asked, confused at my wife's questions.

"I was just being nice. You all need to let that little hood booger go. She's messing with the image of this company. And the fact that she is your assistant makes my skin crawl. How are you going to have her representing you?" she nagged.

"First of all Nova, this is my place of work. Your name isn't Durden and you don't own shit around here. Now hurry up and tell me what you need and get out of my office so I can get back to work. Because ultimately I represent myself. And if I am caught arguing with you in my office that makes me look bad."

"How dare you speak to me that way. I am your wife," she started up again.

"Okay, and be a good wife and get out of my office. I have too much to do today for you to be in here acting like a bitch. If you want to continue to drive fancy cars and eat expensive dinners, let me work," I barked in a low tone. I didn't want anyone in my office to hear me speak to her this way.

"Whatever, Ty. I'm out. And the only reason I came is to tell you that I was going to be working close with your company on a new PR campaign. But fuck you!" she snapped as she marched out of my office.

I let out an audible exhalation as Kinasha climbed from under the desk.

"Who does that bitch think she is?" Kinasha questioned as she straightened her blouse and skirt.

"Just get back to work." I waved her off. I was beyond pissed that my wife had popped up on me. And that she would be working with my company makes things been more difficult.

"What the hell do you even see in her? She is so stuck up!" Kinasha yelled.

"Little girl, why the fuck is you trying me right now?" I barked as I pushed her towards the wall. My eyes burned into hers. I could barely think straight.

Kinasha was just a jump off who didn't know her place. And my wife was going to be in my business, which irritated me. I just needed a moment of silence, yet this trick wanted to start some mess.

"Fuck you, Tyriq! If you keep treating me like this, I will go to HR and tell them about our affair. And then where will that leave you," she threatened before jerking away from my clutch.

Frustrated, she rushed out of my office, slamming the door, causing the awards on my wall to fall to the ground.

This bitch had to go. If a senior executive was around to see this shit, I would be in trouble. I knelt down to pick my awards up and placed them back on the wall before slumping back in my chair.

And when I did, I noticed a text message from Chop, threatening me to get my company to ease up off of The Gardens. I shook my head and deleted the text. That nigga was still trying to behave like a thug while dealing with corporations. Niggas need to know it's a whole other ball game. I just pray he doesn't do anything stupid, thinking he is getting back at me. Because I know where the traps are and I'll gladly get the DEA on that ass.

Chapter 11

Nova

After being disrespected by my husband, I went to lunch alone and then returned back to work. I quickly wrapped up my day and headed home.

The way he spoke to me sent chills down my spine. Never in our relationship has he ever spoken to me this way. I rushed home through the traffic and when I got there I peeled off my clothes and threw on my comfortable robe.

Sashaying around my kitchen, I whipped out a bottle of Moscato and a tall wine glass. Typically, I preferred Riesling, but today I needed something sweeter to combat the bitter taste Tyriq left in my mouth.

The bad thing about Moscato is, it's so delicious it's easy to knock it back. Three glasses of wine later, I was relaxed and stretched out on our sofa flipping through the channels.

I decided to turn on my Roku and go to Hulu so that I could catch up on the latest of Love and Hip Hop Atlanta. I was severely behind. I was curious to know how things ended up with Scrap Deleon and his crazy ass love triangle. That one bitch, Tommie, was psychotic. I couldn't help but be entertained by her crazy going from zero to one hundred in a matter of seconds.

After about two episodes, I checked my phone to see if my husband had at least called me. But he hadn't. My stomach began to growl so I paused the show and went to the kitchen, knowing damn well there was nothing there.

Since my husband wanted to be a dick, I decided to go get dressed again and head out to grab a bite to eat from Sardi's, the Peruvian chicken spot. Tyriq loves their food and all of those delicious sauces they have. I'll order me some and leave it out on the counter to piss him off since he wanted to act crazy with me.

Once I was re-dressed in a pair of jeans and a pink tank top, I rushed back downstairs. Just as I turned my doorknob, I was startled by a man standing on my stoop. He looked as if he were about to knock on my door.

"Who the hell are you?" I asked.

"Are you Nova?" the man questioned. He was older with a head full of gray hair.

"You're on my doorstep asking if I am Nova. Nigga please, get out my way. And get off my property," I snapped as I tried to move past him to get to my car. The grumbling in my stomach overpowered my concentration.

"You are more beautiful than I imagined," his voice cracked.

I stopped in my tracks and turned back around to him.

"What are you talking about?"

"You're Nova, I know you are. You have my nose. You're my daughter," he confessed, his eyes welling with tears.

"My father is dead. So whatever bullshit you are on, you can quit it," I snapped.

The mysterious man walked closer towards me.

"Listen to me, Nova, you are my child. My name is Reginald Hoover and I dated your mother, Antoinette Johnson twenty-eight years ago. I have proof."

What the fuck? How is this nigga going to pop up with this shit? I'm way too hungry for this but I was curious.

I stepped closer to him, looking him in the eye.

"You got some pretty big balls to come around here claiming that you are my father. Are you calling my mother a liar? Because I grew up believing my father was dead."

"I promise you, I am not lying. Here is a picture of Antoinette and I when she was pregnant with you." He handed a tattered Polaroid to me.

There was my mother, looking like she was about to pop, while Reginald draped his arm around her, smiling. My heart began to race as I grew angrier with every exhalation.

"Why would she lie then?" I asked as tears stung my eyes.

"I'm ashamed to say this but I was married to another woman. Your mother knew and she got pregnant on purpose. But I accept my responsibility in the role I played."

I became paralyzed as this man dismantled everything I believed to be true. All of these years I thought my father had died and had no family, when he was alive all along. It felt as if the walls were closing in on me and I had a pair of hands gripped around my neck. I could barely breathe.

"I'm so sorry for not being around," he apologized, stepping even closer. Recoiling, I backed away. Being able to move surprised me since I felt that my knees would buckle at any time.

"Why the hell weren't you around?! Why would Antoinette lie to me?!" I shrieked at the man.

"She was upset that I wouldn't leave my wife. I told her I wanted to be a part of your life, just not hers. She couldn't accept that. I even confessed to my wife about you when you were born. But your mother changed her number and moved away. I've looked everywhere for you and was never able to track you down. Admittedly, I gave up."

The tears that hovered in my eyes fell like heavy raindrops. It was as if my life had been shattered.

"What the hell is going on?" my husband's voice called from behind me. I didn't even hear his tires rolling in the driveway when he pulled up.

"Ty, this is my father." My bottom lip trembled as I stared ahead at the man who possessed my nose and my eyes.

"What?" Ty asked as he moved closer to us.

"I can take a paternity test to prove it," Reginald announced.

"I think that's best. You go get the test and we'll be here," my husband spoke, pulling me away into the house.

After crying into his arms for about five minutes, I finally told Tyriq what Reginald had said to me.

All he could do is plant kisses on my forehead and whisper to me that it was going to be all right.

These years I spent hating my mother were not for nothing. She was truly a rotten bitch.

Reginald came back with the test. We took and then mailed it off to the lab. Now all we can do is wait.

Chapter 12

Skye

"This semester we will be focusing on childhood learning patterns..." My new professor, Professor Gaines, explained the syllabus while the class took notes. I tried to keep focused on her lecture but it was difficult.

Two weeks had passed since I spoke to my mother and I was feeling slightly guilty. We hardly ever fought but I had to stand my ground. She was dead wrong for going back on her promise.

Because of her bullshit I had to apply for student loans and get in debt, which I wanted to avoid. Hell, I don't even have a credit card. I was serious about keeping my credit good and my name clean.

After the stress of securing a loan and dipping into my savings for my books, I needed to relieve some stress. Quan had been texting me a lot this week and finally we were going out tonight.

Since the night I met him, he'd been on my mind. In between filling out loan applications and cursing my mother out in my head, I daydreamed about him wrapping his arm around me and pulling me in close.

He had a sophisticated thug appeal to him that made me wet. He was def the type of nigga that brings out your inner hoe. I couldn't wait to see him.

When he told me he was taking me out, he demanded that I wear something nice.

After class, I rushed home to get dressed for our date. I poured my body in a high waist gold pencil skirt and a white leotard that exposed my back. I slid my French tipped toes in some black open toe stilettos. My hair was pulled in a slick bun while my lips were matte nude and my faux eyelashes were on fleek.

Misting myself with my Chanel perfume, I waited for him to pick me up. While staring at my phone to check the time, Nova called me. We hadn't spoken since she stormed out of my mother's engagement announcement.

Since I was currently mad at our irresponsible ass mother, I picked up.

"Wsup," I asked, while peeping out my blinds in anticipation for Quan.

"Skye, I met my father," she started.

"What are you talking about?" Her father had been dead since she was born.

"Antoinette lied to me! She fucking lied all these years! He's alive! We took a paternity test and did a rush for the results. He came by the other day..." she began to explain.

With every word she told me about our mother being a side hoe, my stomach did back flips. I cringed as the truth came to light. Perhaps what Rico's children said about their relationship was true. She had been fuckin' him while their mother was alive and when she died they made their move to get married.

"Are you there?" Nova asked in between her tears.

"I'm here, sis. I can't believe that bitch! I cannot believe she did this to you, to us!" I yelled. My mother was a hoe who put men before her children. In retrospect it had always been this way. There was always some loser ass nigga around who she did everything for while neglecting us.

"I haven't even spoken to her," Nova admitted.

"What is there to say? She will only lie some more. All she does is lie. I didn't even tell you that she took back her offer to pay my tuition!"

"What the hell? I knew she would do that! How are you going to go to school? What do you need from me? I can help." That's the thing about Nova. We may not always get along, but she is always there for me. Every semester, she gives me about $500 towards my books and extra money for other supplies. She looks out for me like a big sis should. In fact, she actually does more for me than my mother.

When I think about it, Antoinette had never done much for either of us. I was just blindly loyal because she was our mother. I've always pitied her for the way she grew up and thought it wasn't her fault we were poor. But it was. She is a lazy, hoe-ass liar!

"I had to take out a loan," I replied.

"Fuck that, I'm giving you some money this weekend. See if you can cancel that loan. I'll just dip into my equity. I don't want you to start your life behind and be a slave to debt," my sister replied. As bad as I wanted to take her up on her offer, I couldn't.

It was time for me to be independent. I didn't want to end up like Aoki or worse, like my damn mother.

"Nova, I appreciate the offer, sis. I really do. But I can't accept money from you right now. I need to be independent."

"You're so stubborn," she laughed. At that moment Quan knocked on my door.

"Nova, that's my date. Let's meet up this weekend to talk. We have to confront our mother," I said as I hung up the phone.

When I opened the door, Quan stood there dressed in a pair of nicely fit flood pants, a fitted jacket, and a pair of Tom Ford loafers. His shoes cost more than my entire outfit. Actually, it probably cost more than all the outfits I'd worn over the last few days.

"Damn, you look gorgeous," he complimented.

"Thank you. You look good too," I replied.

"Let's get out of here." He reached for my hand, pulling me away. We walked downstairs to his ride, which was a decked out Range Rover.

Opening the door for me, he gave me assistance into the car. He hopped into his side and pulled away from my apartment. While cruising, he turned on the radio and Ro James' "Permission" was on.

"This my shit," he spat as he turned the volume up.

"It is a sexy song."

Butterflies had taken up habitat in my belly. My nerves were such a mess that I couldn't even speak.

"Where are you from?" he asked after the song went off.

"I was born in D.C., raised partially in The Gardens and the rest of my childhood I lived in Oxon Hill."

"You so damn prissy to be from the hood," he lightly chuckled, while stopping at a red light. I was staring straight ahead, but I could feel his eyes burning into the side of my face. Avoiding the awkwardness, I turned to him.

The moonlight brought out the light color in his eyes. They had become hypnotizing.

"I'm not that prissy," I protested.

"That shit ain't a bad thing, shorty. Prissy girls are cool. I can't stand no ghetto bitches. Too damn loud. Always want to throw hands. I'm like bitch, if I wanted to date a loud, violent motherfucker, I'd be with a nigga. I like my women soft," he laughed as he drove away.

"I bet you ain't never even been in a fight," he assumed. It couldn't have been further from the truth. I've been in fights in high school. Lost some, won some. Bitches like to try you when they think you're meek. I used to get picked on for having long wavy hair. They would say that I think I'm cute.

Yeah, bitch, I think I'm cute, but it ain't got to do with hair. It wouldn't matter what grew out my scalp, I would have high self esteem. But since Quan didn't like women who fought, I nodded at his assumption.

"Nope, I don't fight," I lied.

"I figured. You too pretty to fight."

"Where are you from?" I asked to divert attention away from my lie.

"Uptown! I'm from Harlem, B."

"How'd you end up down here?"

"College. Damn, your young ass was probably in middle school when I entered college. I'm out here robbing the cradle."

"I'm legal now," I sassed, while playfully rolling my eyes.

"That's all that matter. I should've asked for some I.D. My man's got caught up with a young bitch once. She was sixteen, had an ass like she was twenty-five. He ended up doing five years for that. "

"That's crazy, but what school did you go to? What was your major?" I probed. He was so fine and I wanted to know more about him.

I loved his New York accent, and the way that he carried himself.

"Are you with the feds?" he joked because of my questions.

"That shouldn't matter if you're not breaking the law."

"True. Well, I went to Howard. I majored in business and currently I'm the CEO and partial owner of a chain of coffee houses called Mocha Hut."

"Oh wow, I've heard of them. They're all over the city. There's one next to my school that I study at sometimes."

"Yep, that's me and my business partner's company. I spend most of my time in our headquarters in Silver Spring. I make my rounds to the other locations. I may have seen you before." He winked.

"Nice. You're an entrepreneur." That would explain why he was paid.

"What do you want to do after you graduate?" he asked as he reached Georgetown, D.C.

"I want to teach English and dance."

"Oh yeah, you did tell me that. What made you get into that?" he pried.

"I love the English language. I like to read and write and I want to give back to my community. I feel like teaching is the best way to do that. I don't want to do it forever. Eventually, I want to publish my poems and stories. And on top of that I am a dancer. I've been in lots of ballet shows."

"Damn, I'm feeling you. You sound like you have a good heart. Teaching is a tough gig. These little niggas these days are crazy."

"I know but someone has to do it or they won't get the help that they need."

"True," he replied when he parked in the garage.

After walking over and letting me out, he placed his hand around my waist and walked me out of the garage to a hotel.

I hope he didn't think that I was sleeping with him. Just because he was fine, doesn't mean he could get my pussy on the first night. No matter how bad I wanted to pounce on his dick, I knew I had to take it slow so that he would respect me.

"There's a dope restaurant on the roof. I have a reservation. We'll overlook the water," he announced when he opened the door for me. I exhaled a breath of relief.

When we arrived to the roof, my nerves began to rattle again. It was a gorgeous view. In all my years of living in the DMV, I had never seen Georgetown from this perspective.

The moonlight bounced off of the dark, rippled river while other lovers strolled by. Colorful flowers decorated the balcony where we sat and soft jazz music played in the background.

"It's beautiful up here," I complimented.

"I only wanted to see you in a beautiful light. You look too good to take to hood-spots, like where I met you."

"I thought you said it was your friend's lounge. Why are you trying to convince me to not go back?" I asked.

"Just because it's my friend's lounge doesn't mean that it's for chicks like you. You deserve to be in the finest places. Not no smoky hookah spot with a bunch of d-boys and wannabe model chicks. Like that girl you were out there with?"

"Who, Aoki?"

"Yeah, whatever her name is. I could tell by looking at her that she was a gold digging thot. I watched her as she looked every man up and down, sizing them up. Trying to see how much they were worth by what they were wearing."

He was wise because he had Aoki down to a science.

"I know you ain't like that. I got that energy from you. And after talking to you, I know for sure you not about that life. But why are you hanging out with her?"

"Aoki isn't all bad. She's a good friend. She used to go school with me. That's how we met."

"Let me guess, she dropped out to dig in men's pockets?" He laughed as the server came over to take our orders.

We quickly scanned the menu. He ordered a Jameson on the rocks and the steak dinner, while I ordered salmon and a drink with mango, champagne, and rum.

I attempted to distract his attention away from Aoki because I cared about her. She had been a good friend to me despite how she carried on with men. As long as she wasn't fucking my man, I could care less what she did.

However, I did like that he was able to read people. He was smart and intuitive. He was much different than that asshole Chad.

"Are you single?" I asked, because you can never be too sure.

"Yeah. I'm about my money right now. Looking for a wifey, though," he replied.

"What about you?" he threw back at me.

"Yep."

"What happened to your last boyfriend?"

"His name was Chad, a thug who was controlling and cheated on me. I loved him so I stayed with him. But when he became stalkerish and borderline abusive, I broke up. But that didn't stop him. He stalked me so bad that I had to move off campus and my grades suffered. Eventually, I lost my academic scholarship..."

As I told Quan more and more about Chad, I could see that he was visibly upset. I could see him turning red while the vein in his temple throbbed. It was sexy how much he cared about me.

"That nigga needs his ass whooped for doing that to you. I'm sorry you lost your scholarship. I can help you with that," he said.

"How? There is no way I can take money from you."

"Not from me. I don't know you like that," he laughed.

"Then how can you help me?" I asked.

"Mocha Hut has a scholarship fund. For some reason, no one applied this year and we have a lot of money to give away. Fill out the application as soon as possible so that it looks legit. I'll get my board to approve it and can cut you a check at least two days after we get the app. Cool?"

My eyes lit up like fireworks. This man was amazing and this was only our first date. He didn't even know me but he cared about my education unlike Chad, who sabotaged it.

And I didn't feel bad about taking that money since it was for scholarships anyway. I was still earning it off my own merits.

"Thank you so much!" I gushed.

"You're welcome, shorty. I like to support black women getting their education. Don't ever let a nigga get in the way of your success. No nigga is worth it."

His advice was heartwarming and well received. For the rest of the dinner, we talked about everything. From our hopes and dreams to our childhoods.

The conversation didn't end there. Eventually, we walked down to the water and sat at the ledge. We dangled our feet over the edge while we talked even more. I told him about my mother, which also pissed him off. I explained to him what had just happened with Nova and my tuition.

"Damn bitch is wild! I can't believe you turned out so well after being raised by her," he barked.

"It's a wonder how me and my sister aren't both crazy."

"She's supposed to look out for you. And here she is choosing some dick over her daughters. How she gon' give a washed up football player your tuition money? That simp should have had some cash saved from his NFL days. I hate bum ass niggas."

"It's so frustrating," I fussed.

"It's cool. You got the Mocha Hut scholarship." He smiled, making me feel better about my mother. However, Nova and I still needed to talk to her.

After the date, he dropped me off without trying to come in. I loved that he didn't try to get some ass but it made me want him even more.

"I can't wait 'til I see you again," I confessed when we reached my door.

"I'll make it happen. And don't forget to apply for the scholarship," he said before planting a light kiss on my lips. My body shivered all over as I watched him swagger away. It wasn't until he reached his car that I opened my door and got in.

Chapter 13

Tyriq

"Where are you heading?" Nova asked me when I walked down the stairs and grabbed my keys off of the mantel.

"It's Gwap's birthday. I'm heading to celebrate with him at the casino out in Arundel Mills."

As soon as I responded, I could see her mood shift. Her posture turned threatening while her brow wrinkled.

"Do you have to go? Can you stay with me tonight?" she asked.

"Babe, I haven't gone anywhere since we found out about your father. I just need a night out, alone. Can I have that?" I stepped closer to her and caressed her cheek.

"Whatever, Ty. It's funny that when I need you the most, you disappear."

"Nova, that's bullshit. I've gone to work and came straight home to you every day this week. How can you say that I'm not here for you? I've been nothing but here for you!" I barked.

"Fuck you! Just get the hell out!" she yelled before stomping back up the stairs. Without fighting back, I dipped out. I needed a break from the drama.

While I sped over to the casino, I blasted Desiinger's "Timmy Turner" to clear my head. Nova was my heart. I loved her more than anything in this world, but this shit with her family was becoming cumbersome. Since we've been together there has been nothing but craziness between her and her trifling mother.

And after listening to her complain about her mother for a week straight, I needed to get out of the house. I don't even understand how she can talk about the same thing over and over again.

I parked in the garage at the casino, and headed into the building to meet up with Gwap. He was one of my homies that I grew up with in the Gardens. That nigga was still one of Chop's hit men. The man wasn't that smart, but what he lacked in brains, he more than made up for in tyranny.

He would take anyone out at anytime for the right price. I was a little nervous hanging out with him considering me and Chop's beef, but I doubt that Chop would kill me. Whether I get my company to back off of the condos in the Gardens or not, I could still be valuable to Chop. And Gwap and I are best friends. Before he would kill me, that nigga would give me a heads up and possibly a head start to get out of town.

"Wsup nigga!" Gwap shouted when I entered the VIP area. He was surrounded by a horde of gorgeous model-looking bitches. It was like a candy store for grown ass men.

"What's good!" I dapped him up.

"Shit. Get you something to drink. We got everything back here. Henny, Ace of Spades, Cuervo, nigga you name it!" Gwap looked lit. His words were slurred while his eyes sat low. I'm surprised he even recognized me. He was nursing a bottle of champagne and I'm sure that wasn't his first drink.

I walked away from him to take him up on his offer. As I made my way through the crowd to the private bar, I made sure to look out for Chop, but he was nowhere in sight. It surprised me that he wouldn't be at Gwap's birthday party, but that's probably because he had some work to do.

"What can I get for you?" the sexy bartender asked me when I approached.

"Remy on ice," I replied, sizing her up. Her skin was a creamy caramel hue, complimented with a pair of chinky eyes, a button nose, and a pair of kissable lips She wasn't wearing a ton of make-up like every other woman in that party, which made her stand out. And from what I could see her body was banging.

"Sure thing," she sweetly replied, while pouring the drink and sliding it over.

I whipped out a couple of twenties to tip her because she was that damn fine. She was actually the baddest bitch in the party. It was crazy that she was working rather than sitting at Gwap's side with the rest of his harem.

"What are you doing? The drinks are on the house." The look of surprise in her eyes was adorable. I chuckled at her response.

"Relax, it's a tip."

"Thank you!"

"No, thank you. What's your name?" I couldn't fight it.

"Aoki. What's yours?" she asked back.

"That's a different name. What's the origin?" I asked, without giving her my name.

"It's Japanese. It's my mother's maiden name."

"Well it's very beautiful, much like yourself. Why your man let you work this late, especially at this type of place?" I pried while sipping the Remy.

128

"If I had a man, I would hope that he wouldn't let me work this late."

"If you were my woman, you def wouldn't have to." What the fuck was I doing? There was only one way this was going to end up. I was going to get her number and eventually we would fuck. That was my pattern. It was a crazy ass pattern that I needed to break.

Things weren't going that great with my wife. And I really needed to end shit with Kinasha. Some new pussy would be nice but I should just be focusing on my wife and my career. But Aoki was fine as hell.

"Sounds nice, but I know how you men are," she rebutted.

"And how are we?"

"Full of shit. For one, you're wearing your wedding ring. For two, you never even told me your name."

Embarrassed, I looked down at my ring and shook my head. Welp, there goes my chance at new pussy. I shrugged it off.

"I'm not full of shit. If you were mine, you wouldn't be out here this late. Just like my wife isn't." I smirked before I walked away with my drink in hand.

"Wait! I didn't say a wife was a deal breaker. I just don't like liars," I heard her say from behind.

Intrigued, I walked back to the bar. It wasn't every day a man hears that his wife is no big deal.

"Liars get on my nerves. But I liked how you didn't bullshit me when I pointed out your ring. So again I ask, what is your name?" She leaned in closer, allowing me to get a whiff of her Dior perfume.

"Tyriq," I replied.

"Here's my number." She wrote it down on a napkin before sliding it across to me.

I slipped it in my pocket.

"Go have fun at your friend's birthday party. We'll talk later." She winked.

"I look forward to it."

I returned back to the party, where Gwap was pouring a bottle of champagne on some chick. I couldn't help but laugh. This nigga was wild.

While I chatted up some of my other homeboys, I received a text message from Kinasha, begging me to come over. I told her no but she kept threatening to tell HR. I had to do something about her. And I had to do it quick.

Chapter 14

Nova

A bottle and a half of Reisling coursed through my veins. I sat on my chaise lounge chair in our bedroom while wearing nothing but a robe. I was drunk, angry, and sad. I knew that there was something was going on with my husband but I wasn't sure exactly what it was.

It was 3:00 am and he still wasn't home. He had left about 11:00 pm but as a married man that is way too late to be staying out. It was inconsiderate of him to leave me like this, especially since he knew what was going on with me. That nigga had to be cheating. Why else would he be coming home late and being so mean to me?

Despite my wrath, my eyelids became heavy and I started to drift to sleep. But I was awoken when I heard our alarm sound and the front door open. He was probably betting on me being knocked out which is why he came home so late.

But I perked up when I heard his heavy footsteps climb the stairs.

"Who is she?" I asked as soon as he stepped his foot inside the room.

"Not this shit again. Take your ass to bed," he snapped as he walked further into the room. The lights were off and I all I could see was his shadowy figure moving about.

He reeked of liquor and cigar smoke. The stench turned my stomach upside down.

"Don't think you're getting in my bed smelling like that. You need to take a shower or sleep in another room," I threatened.

"What the fuck is your problem. It's after three in the morning. Why are you still up picking a fight?!" He had the audacity to question me.

"Because you are fooling around. So who is she?!" I jumped from the chair and raced to where he stood. He flipped on the lights, blinding us both. When my eyes finally adjusted, I looked into his. They were bloodshot and pulsing with anger.

"I don't know what the fuck you are going through, but you need to calm your ass down. I'm not cheating on you. I work hard, damn it! I work to make sure you can have whatever the fuck you want. I don't have time to run around with random bitches. I'm doing all of this for you."

"You're a damn liar! Let me see your fuckin' phone!" I thrashed.

"Here!" He handed it over with ease.

"Go through it so you can see that you are crazy. I work hard and the one night that I went out to party, you accuse me of cheating. All you want me to do is work and lay up under you!" he shouted while I scrolled his phone. I went through pictures, text messages, and phone calls. I even searched to see if there were hidden apps that help you cheat. There was nothing. My anger began to descend into shame and embarrassment. I had fussed him out and accused him of the unthinkable. When the truth is, he had been there for me.

Tears filled my eyes as I hung my head in shame before handing the phone back over.

"That's what the fuck I thought," he sneered before tossing his phone on the dresser.

"I'm sorry," I apologized as a lump formed in my throat. It was hard to speak over it and no matter how hard I tried, I couldn't swallow it.

"You should be. You've been acting like a bitch and I've been there for you. I gave you a necklace I could barely afford. I take you to nice places. If you didn't want to work, you know I would take care of you. I'm grinding to get this promotion so that I can be in a better place to have a baby. But all you fucking do is nag me! Bitches would kill to have a nigga like me!" he ranted, making me feel even worse.

"I know baby. I'm so sorry. It's just this shit with my mother and meeting my father has made me feel crazy. You are a good man, Ty, and I need to do better at showing you that I appreciate you." I moved closer to him, and caressed his arm. Out of fury, he jerked his body away from me.

"Don't fuckin' touch me. I'm sleeping in the guestroom tonight." He turned and walked away but I stopped him by pulling at his hand.

"What the fuck do you want now?!" he asked, looking exhausted.

I bit down on my bottom lip and dropped to my knees. I knew what I needed to do. It was rare that I gave him head but it was necessary tonight.

"You don't have to do this. I know we're both tired," he protested but I wasn't having it. I undid his belt and jeans, sliding them down to the ground.

Without hesitation, I slid his dick in my mouth. I could feel the tension leaving his body as I wrapped my lips around his shaft. I bobbed my head back and forth, as I made slurping sounds.

I'll be the first to admit, sucking dick isn't my forte. But I will do whatever it takes to make it up to my man. If he liked it, I was going to learn to love it. I tried my best to deep throat him but choked.

That didn't stop me. I continued to please my man, sucking and licking all over his dick. He placed his hand to the back of my head and before I knew it, he came in my mouth. I squeezed my eyes tight as I swallowed his essence. After his eruption, he wandered to the bathroom and crawled into the bed where I met him. We slept in peace for the first night in a long time.

Chapter 15

Aoki

Niggas are easy. All I had to do was smile at that nigga Tyriq and he fell into my trap with ease. This is why I will never get married or settle down with one nigga. They all cheat. And his dumbass wife is sitting at home somewhere, thinking he is faithful. Dumbass.

Skye and I sat in Chanel's Nail salon, getting our manis and pedis. We both had dates tonight. Mine was with Tyriq, hers was with that man she met at the club. He was sexy but Skye was stupid for dating him just because she liked him. She needed to see what she could get out of that nigga before he cheats on her or reveals he has a girlfriend or wife.

"Where are you and Quan going tonight?" I asked while the nail technician exfoliated her feet.

"Not sure. He's into surprising me. I can't fake. I love it!"

"Sounds like that nigga is controlling."

"What do you mean?" she asked.

"You've been on multiple dates with him and he never lets you choose where you want to go.

Sounds like he is trying to make sure you don't end up anywhere his wife or girlfriend will be," I instigated.

"Are you serious right now? Do you always have to be so negative? All men are not the same!" she yelled.

"Calm down, bitch. Why are you getting so loud in here? It's embarrassing." I giggled.

"I'm tired of your shit. You are a miserable bitch," she snapped. Just as she went off on me, her toes were done. She jetted out of the chair and went under the heat lamp. I could see her texting someone ferociously. Why the hell was she so upset? She was the one who was more than likely getting played. And she needed to calm the fuck down since I was her ride.

I simply smirked and continued getting my nails and toes done. By the time I sat under the heat lamps, she was getting up and heading to the front to pay. Where the hell was she rushing to?

After she paid she stepped outside but didn't come back in. Once my nails were dry, I called her but she sent me to voicemail. This bitch had lost her mind. I decided to text her.
Me: Where are you?

Skye: My man came and picked me up. I don't need to be around your negative energy anymore. Have a good life.

Me: You petty bitch! Don't call me crying when you get played!

I blocked her number and shoved my phone in the bottom of my purse. Skye was naïve as fuck and it was just a matter of time before it caught up to her again. And I do care about her as a friend, but fuck it. Bitches come and go.

I paid for my nails, and hopped in my fly ride. I went back home to prepare for my date with Tyriq.

Chop was paying me to fuck with him and screw up his life. Chop wasn't sure how to completely go about it so for now, I was just supposed to get him addicted to my pussy. Apparently Tyriq is a dog and has a weakness for pretty women. My job wasn't going to be that hard. I just needed Chop to hurry up and figure out what he was going to do.

I planned on fucking Tyriq tonight. I needed him to be into me quickly. There was no point in taking it slow. I wasn't trying to be wifed. Three dates and 90 day rules are for dumb bitches who want titles. Little do they know, the nigga fuckin' someone else if he's not getting it in with them.

Once I was dressed in a silk black romper that stopped at the knee, exposing my sexy calves, I slid my feet into a pair of silver Loubous. Those $800 shoes were courtesy of ADA Xavier. I sort of miss his ass. He would give me whatever I wanted, whenever.

While I waited to leave my house to meet Tyriq, my cell phone buzzed. It was Xavier. Speak of the devil.

He texted me.

Xavier: Where have you been? I need to see you.

Me: It's over. I don't want to be with a man who is married.

Xavier: I'll leave her for you. I miss you. I love you Aoki.

Me: I don't want you to leave your wife. She and those kids need you. I can't do this anymore.

I had broken up with him the day Chop told me to, but X wasn't handing it well. This nigga had lost his mind, talking about how he would leave his wife for me. I don't want him on a full time basis. And I damn sure don't want to be stepmom to his legion of brats.

I slipped my phone back into my Dior bag after blocking his number. There was no point in letting him have access to me any further.

Tonight I was meeting Tyriq at a club on H Street called Red Room. I was surprised at his boldness for meeting his soon to be sidepiece in public. Before heading out to meet him, I took one more glimpse at myself in the mirror. I had blown out my hair so that it was bone straight, cascading down my back. My lips were a sinful shade of red, complimented by a smoky eye.

Once I was ready, I stepped out of my house and headed to my whip. I drove to H Street and luckily found a parking spot right in front of the club. I considered this a good omen. When I stepped out of my ride, I saw Ty waiting by the entrance.

"Damn, you look good," he complimented as I stepped closer to him.

"Thank you. You don't look bad yourself," I replied. He had a pair of Balmain jeans and Guiseppe sneakers on. The pants and shoes went well with his crisp black V-neck, which exposed his muscles. I also noticed he wasn't wearing his wedding ring. This man was too damn fine for his wife to have ever thought that he would be faithful.

He paid my way into the club and we rushed our way to the bar.

"What you drinking?" he asked, whipping out some cash in a platinum money clip.

"Cuervo and sprite with lime please." I was a simple girl who didn't need any fancy drinks.

He ordered my drink and a Heineken for himself before walking me into a dark corner in the club. The area was secluded since most of the club goers were in the center of the dance floor.

"How are you able to come out here tonight? You aren't worried someone would see you and tell your wife?"

"She knows I'm at the club. If anyone sees me with you, it's easy to deny it. People are drunk and its rowdy in here. You can't trust your own eyes," he responded.

I found him disgusting. These niggas have zero regard for their wives.

"Why do you cheat?" I asked him over the blaring of the speakers.

"That's not important. Why are you single?" He tried to change the subject.

"That's not important either," I replied.

We both laughed it off. I turned around and backed up onto him, twerking on his dick, hoping to feel something. As I backed my ass up on him even more, he brought his hands to my waist, gripping me hard.

I licked my lips as I continued grinding to the Rae Sremmurd and finally, I could feel him getting hard. The girth of his dick pressed against my shorts caused my pussy to get wet. He was packing. I wonder if he knew how to lay it right, though.

I tilted my head back and rested it on his shoulder while he kissed my neck. His masculine hands glided all over my body, causing me to feel tingly inside. I wanted to fuck him. It had been too long since I had gotten some dick. Just as I was about to suggest that we leave, I looked up and saw a familiar face at the bar...

Chapter 16

Skye

What Quan said about Aoki was true. She was a negative bitch who couldn't stand to see anyone else happy. I can't believe the way she acted at the nail salon. Thankfully, Quan had been gracious enough to give me a ride home.

"I hope I didn't interrupt your afternoon too much." I interrupted our silence.

"Nah, I had just wrapped up work. Your nails look nice." He smiled at me as he cruised down the street.

"Thank you. And I forgot to tell you that I got the scholarship check and paid my tuition. I had to cancel the loan first. I started classes last Monday."

"Congratulations. I'm glad my company could help you out."

"Yeah, this is a big help. So, where are you taking me tonight?"

"It's a surprise," he flatly replied.

"I was wondering if I could choose the place. You always surprise me and I wanted to know if I could pick a place tonight." What Aoki had said to me had struck a nerve. Why was he opposed to allowing me to decide where we went out?

"If you want, you can choose it. But what's the big deal?"

"Nothing, Aoki brought up a good point..."

"Are you serious right now? You are telling me that thot who just blew your whole afternoon had a good point? A good point about what?"

Immediately I felt stupid for bringing her up.

"It's not important. It's just, I really want to check out this club on H Street," I announced.

Sighing, he replied, "We can go there."

"Are you mad at me?"

"Nah, shorty. But you gotta think for yourself. Your friend doesn't have your best interest at heart. You can't listen to that hoe. And I told you last time that you need to stop hanging with that bitch."

"I know and you were right. I'm done with Aoki."

"Good," he said as he pulled in front of my building.

"I'll come pick you back up around 11. Wear something sexy and pack an overnight bag." He winked at me before pulling off.

Frustrated, I climbed the stairs to my apartment. I had to get Aoki's voice out of my head. She turned out be wrong anyway. He allowed me to pick a place, thus he's not trying to hide me.

When I went into my apartment, I noticed I had several text messages from my friend Trish. She was a cousin of my ex, Chad.

Trish: Chad was murdered last night!

Me: Wow. I'm sorry to hear to that.

Trish: Come through, his mother would really like to see you.

Me: I can't do that right now. I'll stop by tomorrow.

The truth is, I had no intentions of stopping by. Hearing that Chad had been killed was a relief. After all that he put me through, it felt good to know that he would no longer be around to stalk me or hurt me. A part of me felt sad, because at one point, I did love him. And I know that his mother cared about him deeply. I'd keep her in my prayers.

As for now, I was going to live my life and go on my date with Quan.

***

At 11:00 pm on the dot, he was outside waiting for me. I checked my reflection one more time and was impressed with what I saw. Despite rocking a cheap outfit, I looked cute. I was wearing a zebra print mini-dress and a pair of knock-off Loubous. They had a red bottom, and in the dimness of a nightclub, I doubted anyone would be able to see the difference.

My wavy hair was freshly washed and tossed over my shoulder. My make-up was minimal except for eyeliner, realistic eyelashes, and neutral lip gloss. I preferred to look as natural as possible because I never wanted to be one of those women that men make jokes about taking swimming on the first date.

If you took me swimming right now, I'd look generally the same once I emerged from the water.

I grabbed my overnight bag, packed with toiletries, tomorrow's clothing, and some lingerie. I even had my own condoms because I knew exactly what was going to happen.

"You look good," he complimented when I approached his car. Like a gentleman, he got out and opened my door for me.

"Thank you," I replied when he hopped back in the driver's side.

"Remember I told you about my ex?"

"Yeah, why?"

"His cousin just texted me and told me he was murdered last night. That shit is crazy."

"You said he was a dealer, right? Getting shot is par for the course," he flatly said without an ounce of compassion.

"Damn, that was cold."

"Why does it matter? He made your life a living hell. And why are you even in communication with his family members?" he questioned.

"She's a friend of mine. And it doesn't matter, it's just that a life was lost. You sound indifferent."

"I am indifferent about niggas I don't know and niggas that hurt women I care about. Why would I give a fuck about him? It only means that you are safer now, right?"

"True. Which was a big relief, because I fully suspected that he would made this school year hard as well."

"Well, there you go. There's nothing to worry about," he quipped while driving to H Street.

We had a challenging time finding parking since it was so late in the night. We parked around the corner from the club on a poorly lit street. Although the area was being revitalized there was still a lot of crime that went down. But I could tell Quan could hold his own.

He wrapped his arm around my waist as we walked towards the club. When we got there, I saw a silver Mercedes that looked like it was Aoki's car sitting in the front. I secretly prayed that it wasn't Aoki's ride. She was the last person I wanted to see.

Apparently Quan knew the bouncer because when we stepped to the front door, he let us in without paying the cover or sending us through a security check.

"Let me guess, you have a friend that owns this place too?" I questioned when I whispered in his ear. My lip lightly touched the rim of his ear.

"Yeah, I do. And if you do that again, I'm going to make him let me use his office," he joked before playfully slapping my ass.

He walked me up to the bar, where he whispered something in the bartender's ear. Before I knew it, we were carted away to a VIP section above the club. I had never been in VIP before. Typically I was thrust in the center of a club with the rest of the partiers but tonight, we were in an area above the entire place, looking down at the dance floor.

"It's crazy that I suggested this place and you knew the owner." I laughed while dancing close to him.

"There aren't too many urban spots you can go to where I don't know the owner. What do you want to drink?" he asked me, pulling me in close.

"Moscato," I yelled over Rihanna's "Work."

He let me go and walked to the corridor of the VIP area, where a security guard stood. The security guard motioned for a waitress, who quickly brought us drinks. Instead of just one glass of moscato, she brought two bottles with sparklers inside as if it were my birthday.

After blowing out the pyrotechnics, Quan poured me a drink.

"You're not drinking with me?"

"Nah, bae. I like to keep a level head. I gotta know what's going on. Alcohol makes me react slowly and I need to make sure you're safe."

"Am I in danger?" I asked after taking a sip of the sweet wine.

"Nah, but you never know. Niggas act wild in clubs. You can never let your guard down. I got you. Have fun on me," he assured me.

About four glasses and a slew of trap songs later, I had to pee badly.

"Where's the bathroom?" I asked, breaking our sensual trance.

"It's downstairs. I'll get the guard to walk with you."

"That's not necessary," I said, turning away.

"Yes it is. You're not walking around this motherfucker as sexy as you are without security." In my tipsiness, I shrugged it off. Quan was overprotective and I couldn't fake like I didn't like it. I loved it.

I could tell that he cared, unlike some of these other niggas.

I allowed the guard to walk me down the stairs and through the crowd to the restroom. He waited for me outside of the room while I handled my business.

But as I stepped out of the stall, I saw Aoki standing in front of the mirror re-applying her lipstick. When she caught me looking at her in the mirror, she smirked. My entire mood shifted from light and giddy to anger.

The wine had numbed my face but not my anger towards her. Slowly, I stepped to the sink beside her to wash my hands.

"Are you working on a new trick?" I spitefully asked.

"Funny." She giggled sinisterly while slipping the tube of lipstick back into her purse.

"There's nothing funny about prostitution," I quipped.

"There's nothing funny about walking around in cheap shoes, but you're doing it anyway."

"Not all of us can sell our pussy for clothes."

"Right. Some of us just give our pussies away to niggas who claim they like us but don't do anything but cheat on us. Or worse, stalk us so bad that we fail all of our classes."

"At least I'm not a hoe."

"Let's see how long you'll be singing that tune. Oh, and by the way I want my Chanel bag back," she snapped when she walked towards the door.

"If you have as much money as you claim from all the dicks you suck then why does it matter whether you get the bag back," I shouted from behind her, forcing her to turn around. She marched up to me with a look in her eye that I had never seen before. It looked as if she was going to hit me, but I wasn't afraid. I stood my ground and looked her straight in the face.

"This is the only time I will ever give you a pass. After this moment, if something else like that comes out your fuckin mouth to me, your own mother won't be able to recognize you. That pretty face of yours that got whatever simp that is in the balcony paying your way will be a distant memory. Watch yourself, bitch. Up until just now, I considered you my friend, but now you're on my shit list," she spat before turning around and walking back out the door. My fist were tightly clutched, ready to throw a punch at any time, but it wasn't necessary. She didn't even raise her hand. But before she opened the door, she stopped again.

"And lastly, I'd rather know that I'm a hoe than be in denial about it. That nigga paid your tuition, trust and believe that ass is on a leash now."

"It was a scholarship!" I protested. Immediately I regretted telling her about the generous thing Quan did for me.

"Keep telling yourself that." She smirked before dashing out of the bathroom. I left out behind her only to be even more stunned.

Aoki's new trick was Tyriq! She was fuckin' with my sister's husband.

Rage welled within me as I approached them. This was crossing the line. Aoki had gone too far to fuck with family.

"Are you serious, bitch?!" I screamed at her when I finally reached her.

"Oh shit!" Tyriq hollered.

"What the fuck are you talking about?" Aoki asked.

"You're going to fake like you don't know what I'm talking about. You stank ass bitch! This is my sister's husband," I thrashed before punching her in the face, causing her to topple to the sticky club floor.

I attempted to run to her to beat her ass but Tyriq grabbed me by my waist and lifted me away.

"Get your fuckin' hands off of me!" I screamed while scratching at his arm. Unable to withstand the slicing of my nails, he dropped me, where I ran to back to Aoki who was gathering herself off of the ground.

Her lip was busted, bleeding down her chin. We charged at each other, throwing punches.

"You stupid hoe!" I screamed as I attempted to punch her in the head, but she kneed me in my stomach, causing me to crash to the same disgusting ground she just stood from.

"Have you lost your fucking mind? Did you not heed the advice I gave you in the bathroom. Bitch! I don't give a fuck if that is your sister's man!" she yelled as she kicked me in my side before kneeling down to punch me in the face, repeatedly. Ty grabbed at her and struggled to tame her while I laid on the ground, shielding my face for fear that she would come back.

"What the fuck is going on?" I heard Quan's voice bark. My eyes still closed, I could feel him scoop me up and carry me away while bouncers ushered Tyriq and Aoki out of the club.

As Quan walked me to a back area, I could feel that I was limping. Fuck! My knock off red bottomed heel had broken when I fell. That was an insult to the injuries that occurred when Aoki beat my ass. I was sad to say that was a fight I had lost, but at least I could say I stood up for my sister.

"What was that?" Quan asked once we were inside of an office in the club.

"That bitch Aoki is trying to fuck my sister's husband," I cried while rummaging through my purse for my phone. But then I realized when I fell the entire contents of purse had emptied out. There was nothing left in my bag but some make-up and a few dollar bills. My wallet and phone were somewhere out there in the club.

Without thinking, I started towards the door before Quan stopped me.

"Sit your ass down. Where are you even going?"

"My phone and wallet are out there. I need to call my sister."

"Hell no. I'll get someone to find it for you. And if that shit is gone, then we'll have to get you another one. But what the fuck? How are you going to come up in this spot and like a hoodrat bitch!?

"Don't call me that! That bitch is fucking with my sister!"

"Who gives a shit. Save that shit for the streets. You don't fight in clubs. That trifling bitch could have had a weapon on her."

He was right about that. Aoki was known for carrying around a knife. I'm sure the only reason she didn't cut me was because she was caught off guard.

"I'm sorry but that shit is foul. How could Ty do that to her! I have to tell her now."

"No you need to chill the fuck out and calm down before you create drama where there isn't any. First of all, did you see them kiss?"

"No. They were just dancing and talking."

"Exactly. So you're going to tell your sister what then? That you saw her husband at a club dancing and talking. You'll fuck up a relationship over some petty ass accusations that you can't even prove?" he asked me, causing me to rethink what I did see.

He was right, I had no hard-core proof that he was sleeping with her. However, Aoki did say she was going out with one of her new men tonight. But if I ran back and told Nova, would she believe me?

"I just know Aoki. I know how she operates."

"I thought you were classier and smarter than this. If you weren't hanging out with a thot like Aoki you wouldn't know how they operate. If you were smart you would make sure that you had real proof that your sister's husband was cheating. But you don't. So you need to keep your mouth shut."

Just as he said that someone knocked at the door, interrupting our heated discussion.

"Here's the phone and the wallet," a bouncer said, relieving me of the stress of having to get a new driver's license and canceling my cards. That would have been a major headache.

"Thank you," I spoke while taking the items from him.

When I looked at my phone, I could see I had several text messages from Ty, which I ignored.

"You got me questioning a lot of shit, shorty," Quan said while shaking his head in disappointment. My face throbbed from the strikes it endured. I could barely fix myself to say anything but finally I mustered the strength.

"Questioning what? I made a mistake. I'm still the same person."

"Exactly. It seems like you're the same person as Aoki. Birds of a feather flock together."

"I am nothing like Aoki! I work hard for everything I have rather than opening my legs to the highest bidder. I can't help that I flipped when I saw her with Ty. I know how she is so I naturally assumed that she is fucking Ty."

"I hear you. Which is why I said distance yourself from her. No more of that bitch. And if you have any other friends like that you need to let them go. ASAP. I'm a boss and I only fuck with classy chicks. I don't have time for bitches that fight in the clubs. You understand?"

"I do. And it won't ever happen again. How does my face look?" I couldn't help but ask since I had no way to assess the damage.

"It's not that bad. I can give you some ice when we get back to my crib," he suggested.

"You still want me to come over?" I was sure that he would want to send my ass back home.

"Yeah, I do. We need to take you to the spa to help you unwind from this stressful night. And I need to take you shopping because there is no way in hell I want you caught out here in cheap shoes ever again. You look like one of those crazy bitches on World Star fighting and your shoe breaks." He laughed at me as I rolled my eyes.

"Come on, let's get the fuck out of here and get you home," he offered as he walked me downstairs and out the front door.

When we got outside, I could see that Aoki's car was gone, but Ty was still there leaning against a wall as if he were waiting on someone.

"Hey, Skye, let me holla at you!"

"No nigga!" I waved him off as I kept walking with Quan but Ty ran to catch up to us.

"You need to back the fuck up!" Quan threatened him. He positioned himself in front of Ty to block me.

"I really need to speak with her."

"About what?" Quan asked.

"It's okay, Quan, let me talk to him for a second."

"Are you sure?"

"Yeah, I'm sure," I replied as he walked away to give us a moment to speak.

"What were you doing with her?"

"I just met her tonight. We were dancing, nothing more. You have to believe me."

"I have to tell my sister that I saw you. We may not always see eye to eye but we always have each other's back."

"Please don't tell her you saw me," he begged. When I looked into his eyes I caught a glimpse of sincerity but I couldn't tell for sure.

"You know I can't do that. Aoki is known to sleep with other women's men. I can't keep that from my sister."

"Skye, I am not cheating on Nova. I love her more than anything on this earth and you of all people should know that. You've seen what I've been through and what I've put up with. I will do anything if you don't tell her."

"Anything? You can't bribe me. That is my sister!" I could hear the desperation in his voice. Maybe this nigga had something to hide.

"I know that and if you really care for her you wouldn't put more stress on her than there already is. You know what she's been going through with your mother. Why are you going to burden her with some info that you don't even know is true?"

He raised a good point. By now I was exhausted. My face was in pain, as were my feet from the cheap shoes with the broken heel. Many people were exiting the club, staring at us. I was annoyed and ready to go home to spend time with Quan.

"What can you give me to keep my mouth shut?" I asked out of curiosity. I agreed that Nova didn't need to know anything if I had no concrete proof. But he was going to have to give me something in return for my silence.

"I can pay your tuition. I know you've been having trouble with that."

"That's already taken care of."

"Um, help you with rent? Take you shopping? Just tell me what you need and I can make that happen."

My mind twisted and contorted trying to figure out the best thing that I could ask for. Unlike basic bitch Aoki, I wasn't on the quest for shoes, clothes, and cars. I needed shit that could really get me to the next level. And then it hit me. I knew exactly what to ask of him.

"Get me a job at your company. You're an executive, hook me up with a part time gig or an internship. But it must be paid."

"That's it? And then you won't tell Nova?"

"Yep, make it happen ASAP too." I was tired of working at Friday's for those tips. I needed an office job to work on the days I didn't have class.

"Come by my office on Monday and I will introduce you to some folks. We can work on that," he said, seemingly relieved.

I smiled and turned away to meet Quan, who was on the phone cursing someone out. When he saw me approaching him, he ended the call.

"Aight nigga, just make sure you're there at 6:00 am to receive the shipment. Can't have our café goods sitting out in the open," he spat before hanging up.

"Damn Quan, it's damn near 3:00 am and you are on the phone talking business," I joked.

"That's how bosses operate. Money doesn't sleep, so why should I? And did you get everything straightened out with ya boy?" he asked, pointing towards Ty, who was walking down the street in the opposite direction, presumably to his car.

"Yeah, we're fine. I'll keep my mouth shut because my sister doesn't need the added stress right now. But I told him to stay away from Aoki."

"Good. Come on, let's roll."

Worn out, I struggled to walk to his car, and when I got there, I fell asleep on the way to his place.

Chapter 17

Aoki

When I returned back to my apartment I was livid!
I stomped up the stairs and slammed my door
closed before throwing my purse on the ground.
Who did that bitch think that she was to attack me
over some dick? I didn't know it was her sister's
husband and that wouldn't have changed anything.
Money over bitches all day!

I rushed to the bathroom to assess the damage to
my face; there wasn't much. My lip was busted and
I had minor scratches. All of these things could be
covered by make-up so I wasn't tripping. In fact, I
felt great knowing that I won the fight. I'm pissed
that she snuck up on me, though! I should have
been given the opportunity to whip out Betty, my
trusted switchblade.

After cleaning my face and icing my lip, I began to
grow sleepy. It was late or extremely early,
depending on who you asked. I settled into my bed
and placed my phone on the charger, but I was still
pissed at Skye for trying me. That bitch had no
right to come for me, especially not in public.

I decided to send her a quick text message that
read:

Me: Bitch, when I see you in the street, I got something for that ass!

Once sending that threat that I swore I would live up to, I blocked her number. That hoe won't get a chance to respond nor will she see me coming. I will sneak her ass just like she snuck me.

As I drifted off to sleep I received a phone call from Ty. I hit ignore on his call. I didn't feel like dealing with his ass. He was messy but he kept calling.

"What in the fuck do you want?!" I yelled when I answered.

"I just wanted to apologize about tonight. I had no idea my wife's sister would be there. I'm sorry she attacked you. I wanted to know if you got home safely."

"Nigga, I'm safe. But I gotta go. I can't fuck with you any more. Bye." I hung up. Tomorrow morning, I'd call Chop and let him know he can keep his fucking money.

***

BANG BANG!

I was startled by boisterous knocking on my door. I was convinced that it was the police by the sound of it. I jumped out of bed and rushed to put on some sweatpants and a t-shirt. When I looked through the peephole, it was Chop's ass.

"Nigga, what do you want?" I asked when I opened the door, looking at him square in the face.

"Your face doesn't look that bad," he quipped as he eyed me up and down before pushing himself through the front door.

"Get out of my house! I didn't invite you in," I snapped.

"It's funny to see you dressed like this. Any other time you look like you're ready to go to the club. But you're still cute."

"Nigga, did you hear what I just said? Why are you here?"

"I came to check up on you after that fight you had last night?"

"How did you know about that fight?" I asked, looking at him suspiciously.

"Red Room is in my network of places that I run. That's how I know. I saw that shit got pretty bad for you. I just wanted to know if you were okay?"

"Then if you saw what happened you would know that I'm fine. Maybe you should check on the other bitch!"

"She isn't my employee. You are." He smirked before casually leaning against my stainless steel refrigerator.

"I am not your fuckin' employee. I didn't sign a contract and you don't give me any benefits. Besides, I'm done. I'm not messing around with Ty. That nigga is messy," I stated as I shooed him from in front of my fridge. I reached in and grabbed a bottle of water and opened to take a sip.

Chop chuckled at my response as if he didn't believe me. But that was up to him not to believe me. I needed to get back with Xavier or find a new nigga, because messing with Ty was going to be too much of a challenge. I don't like to work hard. And that nigga would be like a full time job, especially if Skye pops up again.

Out of nowhere, he rushed me, wrapped his hand around my neck, and pushed me into a wall, forcing the bottle of water out of my hand and onto the floor. His fingers squeezed so tight around my neck that I couldn't breathe.

"Bitch, I'm going to say this to you only once. Don't fucking misconstrue what I am telling you. You are still my fuckin' employee until I decide we're through. You will call Tyriq and start seeing him again. And you will get the information that I need you to get. Got that?" he asked with an evil glare in his eyes.

He released me so that he could hear my response.

"Yeah, I got that," I breathed as he stepped towards the door to leave.

"But when my brother gets out, you know what time it is!" I yelled after him.

"Silly hoe. You haven't realized that your brother is dead by now?" He laughed before walking out the front door.

But I didn't believe him. I knew that my brother was alive. I could feel it in my heart. Besides, the prison would have told us if he died. Wouldn't they?

Chapter 18

Skye

The sun assaulted my eyelids as it crept through the blinds. I laid in Quan's king size bed alone, wondering where he went. However, as my senses returned to me I could smell bacon frying outside of the room. He was up cooking for me. Before I rushed out to meet him, I reached for my phone to check my messages.

I had one from Ty, begging me to uphold my end of the bargain. And I had another from Aoki, threatening me. That bitch had some nerve. Fucking with my sister's man is a no-no and if she didn't back off, she would have to see me in the streets again.

I gathered myself out of bed and noticed he left a towel and two washcloths for me. He was so damn thoughtful that it made me smile. When I went into the bathroom, I ran the hot water and took a glimpse at my face. The swelling had gone down significantly, thanks to the ice. Make-up would be able to cover the minor bruising. My face was going to be okay.

After I showered, I slipped in a pair of black jeans and a white tank top with a black pyramid in the center. I applied lotion and some perfume and headed to meet him in the kitchen.

"How'd you sleep, shorty?" he asked as he turned the bacon over and slid it on a plate for me. In addition to the bacon was French toast topped with a caramel sauce and strawberries.

"I slept fine, considering everything that went down."

"Good. I figured you could eat breakfast and then we could head out to the mall. We gotta get you fresh. That shoe situation was embarrassing." I blushed at his words.

"Please stop bringing it up." A nervous giggle escaped my lips.

"I will as soon as we get you some new shoes."

I was amazed at how sweet he was and how willing he was to drop money on me without us even fucking. That's how I know Aoki was wrong about everything.

"Your home is really nice. You did really good with the décor," I complimented as I looked around the spacious loft. The luxury home had floor to ceiling windows, white wood floors, and black furniture with gold throw pillows. I had never been in a place so beautiful. He definitely had money because the loft was up in Columbia Heights. I guess the café business was going really well.

"Thank you babe. I had an interior decorator put it together. I ain't into that decorating shit. You feel me?"

"Yeah," I giggled as I forked French toast into my mouth. He handed me a glass of orange juice that I washed down. For the rest of breakfast we talked about his business and how he wanted to expand beyond the DMV. I told him my intentions on getting a teaching internship and publishing a book of poetry.

He was disgusted when I brought up my mother again and the shit she did to me and Nova.

"Damn shorty, your mother ain't shit for that."

"I know, but she means well. She's led a rough life. Eventually Nova will come around and understand why she did what she did."

"You don't have to make excuses for her. She made stupid and bad choices. I just hope that you can learn from them."

"Trust, I have. I don't mess with married men or men with girlfriends. I'm not like that at all."

"That's good. You have to have some standards. I really like that you're trying to do the best out here. But let's go get you some clothes," he suggested.

Minutes later we headed out of the door and went to Mazza Gallerie, where he let me get anything I wanted. I bought several outfits and expensive shoes. Two pairs of the shoes were real red bottoms. He also bought me a couple of handbags from Louis Vuitton as well as a Celine bag.

A part of me felt like giving him some pussy just to say thank you. But that's the difference between me and Aoki. I don't need to share the preciousness between my legs to get nice things.

Chapter 19

Nova

"How was it last night?" I asked my husband when he finally woke up and joined me in the kitchen for a cup of coffee.

"It was fine. Little joint on H Street. I'll take you there next weekend," he offered but he knew that wasn't my scene.

"You know I don't like clubs. I don't like being around all those whores dressed half nakedly dancing to those shitty songs," I replied while sipping from my mug.

"Nova, you never want to do anything that I want to do."

"That's not true. Just because I don't want to go to the club doesn't mean I don't want to do things with you. Why do you always have to go to the extreme?"

"Why can't you just ride with me and do shit I like. I like clubs and lounges. Sometimes I want to go with my wife. Why can't you just go with me!"

"We've had this conversation over and over. I don't go because I don't want to go!"

"Fuck it. I'm tired of this shit!" he yelled before storming out of the kitchen.

I was too exhausted to follow after him and fight. Instead, I went upstairs to my room and put some clothes on. Today I needed to visit my mother anyway so that she could tell me the truth about my father.

As I walked out of our bedroom, Ty walked in, still icy and not speaking to me. I wasn't sure what the cause of the shift in our relationship was, but I knew it wasn't because I didn't want to go to the club. He had known me for years and I never was a club goer. Why did he think that would change all of a sudden?

I stormed out of the room and hopped in my car and drove to my mother's house. When I arrived I could see that her car was there but her new husband's was not. That's too bad, I wanted him to hear about what kind of old hoe he married. Not that it would matter to him, since she was funding his pipe dream.

"Well look what the cat dragged in," Toni hissed when I stepped foot in her raggedy ass living room.

"It's unpleasant to see you too, Toni," I snapped back while closing the door behind me.

Like the irrational bitch that she was, she left the room and went upstairs to her bedroom.

"Where the fuck are you going? I need to speak to you!" I hollered as I climbed the dusty stairs behind her. We stood face to face at the top of the stairs, looking at each other angrily.

"What is it now, Nova? You came over to tell me how horrible of a mother I am? How I ruined your childhood? You know you complain a lot about me, but look at you. You're successful. You have money! So why are you so fucking mad at me?"

"Don't turn this around to be about you! I have success, no thanks to you!"

"How dare you, you little bitch. I raised you all by myself. Your father died and didn't leave you a penny."

All I could do was cackle. She was standing in my face, telling me a boldfaced lie yet again.

"What's so funny?"

"Who is my father?"

"What are you talking about? You know who your father is."

"Let me ask a different question. Who is Reginald Hoover?" I asked with a smirk stretched across my face. I waited for her to respond, for her to lie to me like she always does. But there was no denying it, not this time.

"I don't know who that is." Toni was dumbstruck, with her jaw hitting the tattered carpet.

"Why are you in this picture with him? And why did the DNA test come back to prove that he is my dad?" I asked after digging in my purse for the proof. When I waved it in front of her face like an immature child, she snatched them from me and began to read them.

"You went behind my back and got tested? You went to go find this man after I told you your father was dead? How could you do this to me!"

"How could I do it to you?! How could you do it me? All these years you have been lying to me. And my father was alive and trying to get to know me. You raggedy winch!"

"Don't talk to me like that. Things were complicated. There is a lot you don't understand. And you need to stay away from that man. He can't be trusted!"

"It seems like you're the one that can't be trusted! He didn't lie to me, you lied to me! And you lied to Skye too! You gave her tuition money to that stupid husband of yours. You are never there for us," I barked. I could see tears welling in her eyes. Perhaps something I said finally struck a nerve.

"Don't you talk about my husband that way. He is not stupid. He is building a business that will bring this entire family millions of dollars. Skye knows that I will pay her student loans."

"Yeah right! Your husband is too dumb to make a business successful. He is just a washed up jock that was desperate for some pussy from you. He wanted your money and that's why he married you!"

"Nova, you have always been such an evil child. And instead of being worried about what my husband is doing why don't you worry about your own. Worry about the fact that he doesn't want to knock you up. Worry about the fact that he keeps a secret cell phone in his car!" she revealed, shocking me in the process.

"You're a fucking liar!" I screamed.

"You know I'm right. Why would I lie to you about that? I saw it with my own eyes. You're so concerned about what I'm doing and who your father is that you aren't paying attention to that fine piece of dick you got in your home. He's probably running around with all kinds of little bitches. And you deserve it. You are just like those weak wives of the men I have slept with. You don't give your husband pussy and you treat him like a child. And then women like me have to come in and clean up your mess. We make your husbands feel like men again." She laughed to the top of her lungs, causing rage to run rampant through my veins.

Unable to hold back, I shoved her violently and she toppled down the stairs. On her way down, she screamed as she broke her leg and eventually banged her head against the corner in the wall.

My heart pumped so hard, I thought it would explode in my chest and I also collapsed, landing beside her at the foot of the stairs.

She didn't move, causing me to grow even more fearful. Was she dead? A part of me hoped so because she deserved it, while another part of me hoped she was alive. She was still my mother, after all.

With caution, I tiptoed down the stairs and knelt down to see if she was still breathing. She wasn't. In fact, there was blood everywhere. When she hit her head on the corner of the wall, she really split her wig.

In a panic, I grabbed my purse and rushed out of the front door. I looked around to see if anyone saw me leaving but there was no one outside. Immediately, I jumped in my car and sped away, praying that no one saw me come in either.

I can't believe I just killed my mother but the only thing on my mind was checking to see if my husband really did have another phone.

When I got home he was still in our bedroom, probably still mad at me. Which was good. I had ample time to check his glove compartment. I carried his spare key on my ring so I didn't need to go into the house.

I went straight to his car and opened the compartment. Lo and behold, there was a phone there that I had never seen before. I turned it on, praying that there was no password needed. Luckily, it was unlocked. I guess he was so confident that I would never find it he didn't bother to lock it.

Most of the text messages were from Kinasha, his assistant. I knew that the way he acted at Sax was strange, but these messages explained it all. There were tons of messages between them about their sexual trysts in her apartment and his office.

My stomach turned and flipped in knots as I read the disturbing messages. How could he do this to me? And with a hood rat bitch like Kinasha of all people. As I continued to read the messages, I discovered that he was attempting to break it off.

But she wasn't having it. He had been ignoring her but she was steadily threatening to go to HR and tell them about him. She was threatening to take everything away from him that he earned. My heart sank to my soles as tears streamed down my burning face.

I was livid that he would do this to me. However, I was happy that he was trying to end it. But if this bitch thinks she can ruin my husband, she had another thing coming. I wasn't letting her take away everything that we've worked for. He was about to get a promotion and this bitch would rip that apart.

I had to do something about her and do it before Monday, since her last text message read:

Kinasha: If you don't leave your wife by Sunday night, I am going to HR Monday morning and telling them all about us. I have nothing to lose. I can get another shitty receptionist job. But you on the other hand... you will be fucked. How will you explain this to your wife?

Tears swarmed my face but now wasn't the time to stay stuck in my pain. I needed to take action and I needed to take it now.

Chapter 20

Tyriq

Last night was nuts and I almost lost everything. I prayed hard that Skye wouldn't say shit to my wife because I can't lose her. No matter how I may come off to her, I love her. She is my fuckin' heart. I would not be where I am in life if it wasn't for her.

But the urge to fuck other women remained. And I thought that Aoki would be done with me after last night, but she had just texted me. She was the baddest bitch I have seen in a long time. Unfortunately, I had to chill. I needed to take time and regroup. Therefore, I wouldn't be seeing Aoki any time soon.

Texting her couldn't hurt.

Aoki: Are you okay after last night?

Me: Yeah. Shit was wild. How do you know my wife's sister?

Aoki: We used to be friends. But as you can see she's a little crazy.

Me: Yeah... lol How are you feeling tho?

Aoki: I'm good. I was wondering if you could get away from the wifey sometime this week.

Me: I don't know. Shit got too real last night.

Aoki: That hoe Skye interrupted us. You know I was about to bounce on your dick all night.

Fuck. Just the thought of her pretty ass swallowing my dick made me horny. Right as I was about to respond, Nova walked in the front door. I could hear the alarm go off from upstairs. I quickly deleted Aoki's messages and slid my phone in my pocket.

I went downstairs to greet her to see how she was feeling. And when I arrived, I could tell she was stressed about something.

"Are you okay?" I asked, slowly pacing towards her. Her eyes were red and she looked shook.

"I'm fine." She tore her body away from me and went to the liquor cabinet to grab a bottle of vodka and a shot glass. I watched as she downed two shots of Grey Goose like it was nothing.

"Are you sure? What the hell happened? Where did you go?" I prodded. My wife looked as if she had been to hell and back. I began to fear that she knew about Kinasha or worse, her sister told her about Aoki.

"I hit a rabbit on the way to the store. And for some reason, it shook me up. A nice man came and cleaned the roadkill off my car. I'm fine but just a little shaken. That's all," she reasoned. But it seemed as if she were lying. I couldn't try for more information because before I knew it, she was downing three more shots.

My wife was a lightweight and I knew that drinking like that was going to make her sick.

"Baby stop. No more. I need you to drink some water and I'll run you a hot bath. Okay?" I offered as I pried the bottle of vodka out of her hand.

A single tear slipped down her cheek as she nodded. I walked her upstairs where I sat her at the edge of the bed. My nerves rattled as I went to run her bath water. Why was she really acting this way? I wondered.

And if she knew about the cheating, why didn't she come out and say it. I prayed that she didn't know, but it couldn't stop me from texting her sister.

Me: Did you tell Nova?

Skye: No nigga. I need that internship.

I slipped my phone back into my pocket and wandered back into the bedroom to tell her the bath was ready.

"What's wrong with me?" she asked while staring off into the distance.

"What do you mean?"

"Why have you been treating me so badly? I love you with every fiber of my being. But you've been treating me so horribly these last few weeks."

Her words fell on me like a ton of bricks. It was never my intention to hurt her this way. I knew I had to make it up to her.

"I know, baby. And I apologize. It's not you, it's this fucking job. Gunning for this promotion has been really stressful but I promise to be better."

She only shook her head and walked away from me. She went into the bathroom and closed the door behind me and I could hear her sink into the hot water.

Immediately, I knew what I had to do. I had to cut off those other chicks and just focus on my wife. I texted Aoki back and told her I couldn't fuck with her anymore. Without waiting for a response, I blocked her number and then rushed to my car.

I hadn't checked the phone that I used to communicate with Kinasha in days. I viewed her messages only to be annoyed at the fact that she was trying to ruin my career. She didn't have much evidence to prove that we were sleeping together, so I knew that I could fight it. I could tell HR she was lying to get a promotion or to get back at me for turning her down. Even if she showed them text messages between us, I could still contest it.

Those messages came from my burner phone. Not my work or personal cell phone. She could have been talking to any nigga. I wasn't worried about that little thot. I went back into the house and ordered dinner for my wife. I needed to turn over a new leaf, and I needed to do it fast.

Chapter 21

Skye

After spending the day at the mall, Quan took me back home to my apartment. This man bought so much stuff for me that I couldn't carry it all upstairs by myself. He grabbed a few bags and helped me to my apartment. I felt giddy the whole time. I couldn't believe how amazingly generous he was.

"Thank you for everything," I said before wrapping my arms around him and taking him in for a hug.

"You're welcome, baby girl. I couldn't have you walking around like that. Not if you're going to be out here representing me," he said as he kissed me on the cheek. His gentle kiss sent shivers down my spine, forcing me to connect my lips with his.

While pressed into his body, he ran his fingers through my hair as I pulled him in closer. Our tongues began to tango with one another, making my pussy flood. I wanted him more than I've ever wanted anyone.

His hands traveled up my shirt to unclasp my bra, freeing my breasts from confinement. He lifted my shirt over my head and threw it onto the floor as if it were a nuisance getting in his way. With my breasts cupped by his hands, he began to kiss and lick my neck. I felt like cumming just from his kisses. I couldn't wait to feel his dick inside of me.

He worked his way from my neck to my nipples, swiveling his tongue around my Hershey kisses. I moaned at the sensation while caressing his shoulders.

He undid his jeans and lifted me up before carrying me to my bedroom, where he placed me down on the bed. He quickly undressed, snatching off his shirt and his jeans before throwing them onto the floor. When he took out his dick, my heart stopped. It was the biggest dick I had ever seen. He had a slight curve that I knew would be up in my g-spot. The veins in his rod pulsed as he moved closer to me.

"Come here and suck it," he commanded me, luring me from laying down. I crawled towards him and wrapped my mouth around his dick. I damn near had to unhinge my jaw to fit him in my mouth. How was my pussy going to handle him, since I hadn't had sex since Chad? And Chad was average size.

I did my best to suck him by licking the tip and opening my mouth even wider.

"Shit, that feels good!" he crooned as he placed his hand to the back of my head, his fingers tangled in my hair.

"Hmmmm" I managed to moan despite my face being stuffed with his cock.

"You gonna make me cum too fast with that bomb head," he chuckled, pulling away from me.

I flashed him a seductive smile because it made me feel good to know that I could have that effect on him. Leaning back on the bed, I spread my legs and allowed him to get a glimpse of my bubblegum pink center. The visual baited him into planting his face between his thighs.

I lightly giggled at feeling his beard tickle my inner thighs. He suckled on my thighs, causing me to quiver. The tease only made me yearn for him to place his tongue on my clit. My fingers glided to his skull, but he pushed them away.

"Uh huh, you need to be restrained," he whispered; the vibrations of his voice titillated me at my core. He grabbed a hold of hands and held them together with one of his while slipping his other hand in between my thighs.

He began to finger my pussy with his middle and index finger. I had never been so wet in my life. This man had me soaking all over the bed and his hand and he hadn't even put his dick in me yet.

"Ahhhh shit!" I squealed as he stimulated my g-spot. He chuckled before licking my clit.

My thighs rattled uncontrollably as he sucked and licked my cleft. He devoured me as if I were his last meal and quickly, I began to cum, exploding all over his beard and face. Sweat dripped from my body as I squirted bullets.

When he lifted from me he wiped his face. And smiled at me sexily.

"Ride this dick," he demanded before leaning back on the bed.

Still weak, I got up and straddled him. Despite being high from the intoxicating orgasm I was nervous about riding him. I wasn't that great at being on top. Chad told me that many times. And on top of that, how the hell was I supposed to fit his monstrous dick inside of me.

Shoving my fears to the side, I got on top of him and slowly slid down on his dick.

"It's too big," I whimpered.

"Nah, you got it. Take that shit," he moaned as I eased onto him. My pussy stretched more than it had ever stretched before.

"This pussy is good," he growled, bringing his hands to my hips and forcing me down. He started to pump inside of me, causing my pussy to get even wetter. Eventually, I loosened up some and began to put in work. I bounced up and down on his dick while looking into his eyes. He was in a state of ecstasy.

"I'm about to cum," he muttered, lifting me off of him. "Suck it again for me, baby."

I obliged, taking him in my mouth as he pumped into the back of my mouth. His cream ran down my throat and I loved it. I loved everything about making love to him. He collapsed on the bed and I curled up to him. Together we fell asleep and I was on cloud nine.

Chapter 22

Nova

After drying off my body from the hot bath, I went to get dressed. It had been a few hours since I had killed my mother, and my nerves were a wreck. The vodka did nothing to calm me down. I wasn't sure how I felt yet about killing her. Of course, I didn't mean to. It wasn't my intention but the bitch had it coming.

She's been a shitty mother my entire life and now her bad decisions are affecting me as an adult. Well, me and my sister. I just hope no one saw me leave her house. And where the hell is her husband? Why hadn't he gotten home already to find her? The anticipation drove me crazy.

But I had other fish to fry. I had to do something about Kinasha. I glimpsed at my clock and it was 9:00 pm; that little bitch was definitely still awake, plotting on ruining my husband's career Monday morning.

I decided to head down to Sax, with the hopes that she would be there working tonight. Since she was there the night Ty and I went. I got dressed elegantly. Couldn't let that bitch catch me slipping. I slipped into a tight red dress that reached beyond my knees. It was backless and sexy. I also brushed my hair back and covered it with a curly blonde wig I had bought last year, when I was trying out a different look.

Once I was fully dressed with my face beat, I went downstairs, prepared to leave.

"I got dinner for us. Where are you headed looking like that?" my piece of shit husband had the audacity to ask me.

"Out," I stated without looking his way.

"Where is out?"

"Oh, you can question me, but I can't question you. Good night, nigga. I'm going out."

I left him standing in the foyer with his jaw unhinged, pissed that I would speak to him that way. I didn't give a fuck. How could he fuck that ghetto assistant of his? But as always, I was going to fix the problems he created for us.

Before heading into the city, I grabbed my husband's phone. Hopefully he won't try to contact her before I'm back in the house.

***

When I got to Sax, the place was emptying out. I caught Kinasha standing behind the bar, counting money. Surprise, the bitch can count. I hid in the shadows, hoping that she didn't see me. The restaurant was closing in a few minutes, so hopefully she would be leaving soon.

"May I help you ma'am?" a host appeared out of nowhere and asked me.

"Do you have a catering menu? I was in the area and I saw this place. I just want to know if you cater because I'm planning an office party," I lied to him so that I would seem less fishy.

"Sure, let me grab that for you." He kindly fluttered away and returned with the menu. By the time he came back, she was heading outside. Due to the wig she didn't recognize me. My plan was going to work smoothly.

I went outside as well and got back into my car while keeping my eye on her. Finally, I saw her pull off and I tailed her to her home. My eyes followed her as she got out of her vehicle and went inside. What did he see in her?

He had everything that he could possibly want within me. So why was he chasing this broad? What could she do for him that I couldn't? I looked to see exactly what apartment she went into.

After about ten minutes, I sent a text message from Tyriq's phone.

Me: Hey baby, I know that you're mad at me right now. But I want you. I'm leaving my wife for you. Come meet me at Lou's Bar and Grille so we can talk. I'll be there in ten minutes.

Kinasha: Wow! I knew you would come to your senses. I'll be right there.

And like the thirsty thot that she was, she skipped her happy ass out of the apartment within moments. All I could do was laugh at how naïve she was. Once her car was well down the block, I got out of mine and went to her apartment door.

Cheap apartments were easy as hell to break into. She made it even easier since she didn't put the top lock on. Dumb broad. I finagled with the lock and got in easily using a credit card and bobby pins.

While inside, I searched for a way to rig her apartment so that she got carbon monoxide poison. At least she would go out peacefully, unlike my mother. It was fucked up of me, but that bitch had to go. She was threatening to take everything away from me and I couldn't have that. I had worked too hard and I refused to end up like my mother. Broke and dead without shit.

My mother died for the same reason Kinasha was about to. They were side chicks who didn't stay in their place. They are side bitches who expected more than what they really deserved. My mother married that man after sleeping with him while he was married. Then she gave him her money, hurting my little sister in the process. She deserved what happened to her. She deserved what she did to me and my father.

And Kinasha was no different. These bitches ruin families. They ruin lives and the world would be better off without them.

My mind was racing a mile a minute as I searched for a way to rig the apartment. I couldn't cut the cord of the stove because she would be able to smell the natural gas and probably would call the gas company.

Finally, I discovered her clothes dyer. I remembered inspectors coming to make sure our dryer gas line was intact when I was little because it could lead to carbon monoxide leakage. Quickly, I ripped it out of the wall. I then went throughout her house to close all vents.

I know this seems fucked up but at least she would die peacefully in her sleep, unlike my mother. Once I was done, I locked the bottom lock behind me and headed back to his car. When I got there, I saw that she had called and texted Ty's phone several times.

The bitch is now realizing he stood her up, I cackled to myself as I drove away. It doesn't pay to fuck men who don't belong to you. And soon she will find out.

***

My conscience was at ease despite the horrible acts I had committed today. All I've ever wanted was the good life, and to have two people try to take it away from me meant they had to go. It was either them or me.

When I pulled up to my house, there was a squad car outside. My heart raced quickly, in fear that the cops knew that I had pushed Toni. My palms began to perspire and my stomach turned in knots.

I had to face the music. Hopefully, I could explain that it was an accident.

"Baby," Tyriq said when I walked in the door. He was standing across from two police officers, one woman and one man.

"What's going on?" I asked, pretending to be clueless.

"Ma'am, please have a seat. We have something to tell you."

"What is it? Is it Skye? Is it my mother?" I pried while trying to conjure up some tears.

"It's your mother. Her husband found her dead when he came in the house this evening. It appeared she had fallen down the stairs. She cracked her skull..."

"Please! Don't say anything else!" I wailed as I broke down in tears.

"I'm sorry, baby," my husband said as he held me close while I cried into his chest. It was an award winning performance, if I must say so myself.

I can't explain just how grateful I am that they thought it was an accident.

Chapter 23

Skye

Tears trickled down my face when I arrived at the morgue to view my mother's body. I was with Quan when my sister began blowing my phone up. Graciously, he brought me up here and now I'm distraught. I hated that our last words to each other were not loving words. I was livid that she was giving my tuition money away.

And now, I would give anything to have her back. Her husband and his two kids sat over in a corner trying to comfort him. But I know they didn't like my mother. They wouldn't even acknowledge her as his wife.

"Baby, let me take you back home. You need to get some rest," Quan offered as he extended his arm around me.

Nova and I had just finished viewing the body and we were equally as much of a wreck. I was surprised to see Nova this affected by our mother's death because they were at each other's throat all her life. But then again, that is our mother.

"Yeah, I'm ready. Let me just say goodbye to my sister," I replied before walking away to Tyriq and Nova.

"It's going to be okay," I said to her before wiping her tears.

"I know. It's just so sudden." Her voice cracked as she attempted to speak.

"Is that guy taking you home?" Ty asked me.

"Yeah, he is." Why was he asking me that?

"Be careful," Ty said before I turned around. I was curious as to why he thought I needed to be careful, but I shrugged it off and walked back to Quan.

Quan escorted me out and took me back home. When we got there, he made me a cup of tea and added a little bit of rum to ease my nerves. This man was amazing at how well he was taking care of me. I had only known him for a short while, yet he had been more loving towards me than any man I had ever known.

"Here you go," he said as he handed me a hot mug. I sipped cautiously while leaning against the pillows in my bed.

"My mother was like my best friend." My voice cracked.

"I know baby. And I'm sorry for your loss. I know how it is to lose a parent," he said to me, referring to the fact that he had lost his father a few years ago. He told me once when we were on a date.

"How did you get through it?" I asked as tears showered my face.

"I kept living my life in a way that I knew would make him proud. There were things that he would have expected of me and I made sure that I fulfilled them. That's what you have to do. Live the life you and your mother can be proud of," he said before kissing me on my forehead.

"I have to leave because I have some business to handle early in the morning. If you need me to stay, I can."

"No, don't worry. I need some time alone." I gave him a halfhearted smile. He kissed me again on the cheek before pulling a wad of cash out of his wallet. He peeled off a couple of hundreds and handed it to me.

"I can't take this." I shook my head.

"Yeah, you can. You're going to be missing work and quite possibly school over the next couple of weeks. I want to make sure your bills get paid and that you get fed. Take the money," he asserted. I felt truly lucky to have a man like him.

I kissed him on his lips and he turned and walked away. I slid the cash in my nightstand and turned off the lamp. The rum relaxed me and caused me to swiftly drift into sleep. But I still was depressed about my mother.

Chapter 24

Tyriq

Monday morning came after a very long Sunday. I felt horrible about my mother-in-law's death. Nova was really going through it and it didn't help that I had been mistreating her.

All day Sunday, I spent time with her, helping her sort through her mother's belongings. She and Skye had found her will and insurance policies. Antoinette didn't have much but the house and one of her polices, which was worth $75,000. After the funeral, they wouldn't leave much money left to split.

I think I might suggest to Nova that she give Skye all the money and we keep the house. Skye needs her tuition and Nova and I can rent the house out.

Speaking of Skye, her new nigga was a little suspect. I couldn't put my finger on it, but I knew him from somewhere. I just couldn't put my finger on it.

Even though I was supposed to go to the funeral home with Nova today, I had to go into the office to get a few hours of work done.

On my way there, I braced myself for what was coming. I knew that Kinasha was going to act a fool. She must've have been very fed up with me since she hadn't returned any of my calls since Saturday night, when she told me she was going to tell HR.

But whatever, I can handle it.

When I stepped onto my company's floor, the executive above me called me into his office.

"What's going on?" I asked, even though I already knew what he was about to say.

"I'm so sorry to tell you this. Kinasha's father called this morning and told us she died this weekend."

"What?! What happened?" I began to perspire. I couldn't believe what he was telling me.

"Yeah, carbon monoxide poisoning. She died in her sleep. Her father came over Sunday morning to take her to breakfast, but she wouldn't answer even though he saw her car outside. He used his key and found her. "

"Wow." I shook my head in disbelief. Even though I didn't want to sleep with her anymore, I still wanted her to live a very healthy and happy life. I felt horrible for her and her father, who I know loved her dearly.

She was a daddy's girl, always talking about how much she cared about him. For him to have found her dead crushed me. I left my manager's office, distraught. It was tough getting work done, but I some how managed to be productive before meeting up with my wife.

"Hey, do you have a second," my manger asked when he knocked on my door. Concern riddled my face. What now?

"Sure," I replied.

"I had to call a temp service to get us someone new at the front desk. She'll be working here until we figure some things out. Come, Aoki," my manager said, causing a lump to form in my throat.

That name was too distinctive for there to be more than one running around. And when she walked through the door, my fears were confirmed. It was the sexy ass Aoki that I went out with the other night.

"Aoki, this is Tyriq," he introduced us. Our hands melted into one another as she stared me in my eyes seductively. I was dealing with too much outside of work to deal with this. And I knew that she wasn't going to make it easier.

Chapter 25

Nova

It's been a week since my mother has been dead and it still seems unreal to me. Sometimes I can't believe I'm the one that did it. Either way, it was time to move on. She was a chronic side bitch and it affected everyone else's lives. She essentially killed Rico Barnes's wife with the stress she caused her. She lied about my father being dead and was trying to ruin Skye's education. Good riddance.

As I drove up to the church where my mother's funeral was being held, I turned on the radio.

"...Woman was found dead a week ago from carbon monoxide poisoning. Autopsy reveals she was ten weeks pregnant. Please remember to check the batteries on your detectors to prevent..."

I damn near swerved off the road after hearing that my husband got her pregnant. That was crossing the fucking line! All this time he wouldn't impregnate me, yet he'll sit up here and bust in this little bitch! Tears began to fill my eyes as I drove up the road. I wasn't sure how to react to him when I saw him, so I figured I would keep busy at the funeral.

I'll avoid him as much as I can. Because if I don't, I might kill him too. That was humiliating. He got her pregnant before me.

***

Right before the funeral...

"Baby, what is going on? Are you okay?" he asked, stroking my cheek.

The touch of his fingers to my perfectly beat face made my skin crawl. I had half a mind to bite him.

"Get your fucking hands off of me," I snarled between gritted teeth.

"I know that you're grieving. I know that you're upset and that's okay. I need you to let it out. Let it all out. You know that I'm here for you," he attempted to convince me. But I knew it was all lies and bullshit.

"Tyriq, get the fuck out of my face. Why are you even here?"

"Nova, I love you! I loved Ms. Toni. She was like a mother to me. Why are you being like this? What has gotten into you? You were fine when I saw you this morning."

"It's funny how quickly someone can change. Isn't it?" I asked cryptically before turning to walk away.

Yeah, I was fine when he last saw me earlier this morning. But that was before I found out the truth about him. A truth that I have to sort through along with the burial of my mother.

As I walked away from my husband, I weaved in and out of the sea of folks dressed in black. I was the only one that dared to wear a light color, aside from some of the children.

My blue dress stood out as I climbed the stairs to the church. I could feel the dozens of eyes burning into my backside as I approached the church's door. When I walked back in, my eyes landed on Skye, who was sprawled out on the closed part of the casket. She was banging her fists on the hard cover while yelling, "Please don't leave me."

I sighed while watching the pathetic sight. You see, this is why I can't mourn. This heffa was doing more than enough.

She hollered to the top of her lungs as a couple of our cousins rushed to her side, attempting to pull her away. The veins in her balled fists throbbed while her tears poured.

She was a sad weakling, just like our mother.

Tyriq rushed past me to pull her away from the casket and sit her down. I decided to join them since it looked shady of me to be standing on the side. I didn't want anyone to suspect me of anything. So I sat on the other side of my sister, cradling her near me. All the while giving my husband an evil eye.

The pastor began the service, but my mind was still somewhere else. All I could think about was Ty getting Kinasha pregnant. I barely noticed when her fake ass ex-husband showed up. This nigga was late to the funeral and absent for the planning of it. Skye kept telling me that Rico loved our mother, so ask him to be involved.

This nigga never responded to my text messages or calls. Instead, he is suing my mother's estate so that he can get the house and her insurance money. She did all that creeping around with a married man for him to only try to screw her in the end. He didn't even offer any money towards the funeral.

All I could do was sigh as I continued to listen to the eulogy. All of this was messy.

Chapter 26

Skye

It had been a week since my mother's funeral and I was beginning to return to normal. Accepting that she was gone was a challenge but I was determined to get through it. I had to take Quan's advice and live my life in a way that would make her proud.

And since her death, there has been a heap of drama with her husband. This nigga wanted the house and the money, which was not going to happen. For all we know, he pushed her down the stairs. He was the one that found her and it's not like my mother was clumsy.

Despite the family drama and grieving my mother's death, I needed to get back on the ball with school. Today I was going to one of the Mocha Hut locations by my school to meet up with a classmate named Phonte. Phonte had agreed to take notes and record lectures for me so that I didn't fall behind.

I met him a couple of years ago in school and I always knew he had a little crush on me, but he wasn't my type. He was too scrawny and I liked my men muscular, like my bae Quan. Even though we never dated, he had been a pretty good friend when it came to school work.

Last year he had surgery on his ACL and I took notes for him, so this time around, he was there to help me.

I parked my car in front of the café. I had never been to this particular location, but this one was a midway point for Phonte and I. The thought of running into Quan here crossed my mind since he owned the chain. But according to him, he mostly spent time at his headquarters out in Silver Spring.

Speaking of Quan, things were going well. He had truly been my rock through this entire ordeal with my mother. I couldn't have wished for a better man. He was sexy, his pipe game was on point, and he was wealthy. The nigga had no problems dropping money on me. I could honestly say I was falling in love with him.

"Wsup Fly Skye!" Phonte greeted when I walked through the door. He threw his arms around me in a friendly hug.

"What's up with you?" I asked, breaking away from him before sitting across from him.

"Nothing much. I got you a vanilla latte with soy milk, just how you like it," he said, pointing at a cup on the table.

"Thank you so much! That was really sweet of you."

"It's the least I could do. How are you holding up?"

"I'm getting there. I'm taking it one day at a time."

"That's good. Here are the notes and recordings from the lectures." He handed me a notebook and a recorder.

"I'll listen to the lectures and get this back to you as soon as possible. You don't know how much of blessing this has been."

"Take your time, Skye. I don't need it back. I was there. I remember everything." He laughed.

"Okay, I'm going to hold you to that."

"Whatever happened to that girl you used to hang with, Aoki?" he asked me, souring my mood in the process. I hadn't thought about that bitch in weeks.

"Hell if I know. We aren't friends anymore. Why?"

"I was wondering if you could put in a good word for me. She was pretty. Not as beautiful as you, but you know she was bad." He grinned.

Jealousy slapped me in the face as I heard him express attraction to Aoki. But it shouldn't have mattered. For one, I had a man. And secondly, I had been turning him down for the last couple of years. Therefore, I had no reason to be jealous.

"Find her on Facebook, because we don't speak anymore." I wrinkled up my nose in annoyance.

"Skye and Phonte?" I heard a woman say our names, breaking the jealous trance I was in. When I looked up, I could see that it was Professor Gaines standing above us.

"Hi Professor Gaines," we both said in unison.

"How are you doing, Skye? I'm so sorry to hear about your loss. Whatever you need from me to help you complete this semester, let me know and I will work on it."

"Thank you Professor Gaines. I'm really working on staying on top of my studies. Phonte has been taking notes and recording lectures."

"That's amazing. I expect the best from you two. You all are some of my best students."

"Thanks," Phonte replied to her compliment.

"What brings you here? Are you grading papers tonight?" I asked, while pointing to her briefcase.

"No. I'm helping my husband do some inventory tonight," she replied.

"Your husband manages this place?" Phonte asked.

"No, he owns it. He owns this entire chain," she said proudly with a smile that stretched from ear to ear.

Her husband owned it? Did Quan lie to me about owning these restaurants?

"In fact, here he is now. He just walked in. Baby, come here," she said, waving her husband over. And when I turned to see who it was, my heart shattered in a gazillion pieces.

I felt like vomiting and passing out right then and there. Her husband was the man I was falling in love with, Quan.

"These are my students Skye and Phonte. They are some of the brightest young minds I've had come through my classroom." She spoke highly of us. But my tongue was paralyzed. I couldn't even speak.

"Nice to meet you," Quan said, extending his hand to Phonte first before he shook mine.

He looked right through me, like he didn't even know me. If it weren't for the fire burning in me, I would have cried. How could he do this to me? How could I not know? I had spent the night at his place several times. He called and texted me all hours of the day. He spent a lot of money on me. It never dawned on me that he would be married.

What the fuck?! Was Aoki right? Are all men cheaters? And I was the stupid bitch getting played...

To be continued...

Want to know if Skye forgives or seeks revenge against Quan?

Will anyone find about Nova committing murder?

Does Aoki finally hook Tyriq?

Find out in the next episode of Ashes to Ashes, Dust to Side Chicks!

Visit 5starlit.com for details on the next book as well as how to win an Amazon Gift Card

About N'Dia Rae

Rae is a 30-something year old living and writing in the DMV. When she's not behind her laptop typing dramatic stories about complexed characters, she's in her kitchen whipping up delicious food. As a rising author she looks to various writers for inspiration such as Shonda Rhimes, Terry McMillan and Zane. Follow her on her journey of unraveling twisted stories for your pleasure.

38277224R00121

Made in the USA
San Bernardino, CA
02 September 2016